ERIN JOHNSON

A BITTER BLEND

A MAGICAL TEA ROOM MYSTERY

GET YOUR FREE PREQUEL SHORT STORY!

It's All Hallows Eve, and the fortune-telling festivities abound at a magical party near charming Bath, England. Only no one predicted that the coven leader would be poisoned! Now, new witch, Minnie and her vampire bestie, Gus, must catch the killer before Gus's secret gets out.

Download Once in a Brew Moon for FREE to solve a mystical murder today!

OTHER BOOKS BY ERIN JOHNSON

The Magical Tea Room Mysteries
Minnie Wells is working her marketing magic to save the coziest, vampire-owned tea room in Bath, England. But add in a string of murders, spells to learn, and a handsome Mr. Darcy-esque boss, and Minnie's cup runneth over with mischief and mayhem.

Spelling the Tea
With Scream and Sugar
A Score to Kettle
English After-Doom Tea
Steeping Secrets
Save the Last Dance for Tea
Steep With One Eye Open
A Bitter Blend
Tea Die For

The Spells & Caramels Paranormal Cozy Mysteries
Imogen Banks is struggling to make it as a baker and a new witch on the mysterious and magical island of Bijou Mer. With a princely beau, a snarky baking flame and a baker's dozen of

hilarious, misfit friends, she'll need all the help she can get when the murder mysteries start piling up.

Seashells, Spells & Caramels
Black Arts, Tarts & Gypsy Carts
Mermaid Fins, Winds & Rolling Pins
Cookie Dough, Snow & Wands Aglow
Full Moons, Dunes & Macaroons
Airships, Crypts & Chocolate Chips
Due East, Beasts & Campfire Feasts
Grimoires, Spas & Chocolate Straws
Eclairs, Scares & Haunted Home Repairs
Bat Wings, Rings & Apron Strings
* Christmas Short Story: Snowflakes, Cakes & Deadly Stakes

The Pet Psychic Magical Mysteries
A curse stole one witch's powers, but gave her the ability to speak with animals. Now Jolene helps a hunky police officer and his sassy, lie-detecting canine solve paranormal mysteries.

Pretty Little Fliers
Friday Night Bites
Game of Bones
Mouse of Cards
Pig Little Lies
Breaking Bat
The Squawking Dead
The Big Fang Theory

The Winter Witches of Holiday Haven
Running a funeral home in the world's most merry of cities has its downsides. For witch, Rudie Hollybrook, things can feel a little isolating. But when a murder rocks the festive town, Rudie's special skills might be the one thing that can help bring the killer to justice!

Cocoa Curses
Solstice Spirits
Mistletoe Mojo

Magical Renaissance Faire Mysteries
Turkey legs, ale, and murder! Is this supernatural Ren Faire cursed? If you like snarky animals, bold heroines, and a hint of romance, you'll love this humorous paranormal cozy series.

Much A'Broom About Nothing
The Taming of the Broom

Special Collections
Spells & Caramels: The Complete Series Boxset

The Spells & Caramels Boxset Books 1-3
The Spells & Caramels Boxset Books 4-6
The Spells & Caramels Boxset Books 7-10

Pet Psychic Mysteries Boxset Books 1-4
Pet Psychic Mysteries Boxset Books 5-8

Winter Witches of Holiday Haven: The Rudie Collection Books 1-3

Want to hang out with Erin and other magical mystery readers?
Come join Erin's VIP reader group on Facebook: **Erin's Bewitching Bevy**. It's a cauldron of fun!

1

THE WELLNESS RETREAT

White sheep dotted the rolling green hills and lush woodland that stretched out for miles. Bumping along the dirt road through England's pastoral paradise, I had to pinch myself to believe that this was really my life. A decade ago, I was sweltering in the brown Phoenix deserts, but now? I grinned out the car window, my spirits lifted by the sense of space and verdant nature all around us.

Gus leaned back in his leather seat, one hand lazily on the steering wheel. The gorgeous countryside and crisp, early spring weather seemed to have even my typically detached bestie grinning.

I shot him a bemused look and adopted a lofty British accent. "Gustaf, I daresay you're looking forward to this country retreat. I didn't think something so rural would be your style."

Fitz chuckled in the back seat.

My blond friend shot me an arch look, then recomposed his features into their normal aloof expression. "This place is supposed to be luxurious, right? You know, expensive is *definitely* my style."

I grinned. He had me there. My vampire bestie's townhouse was all gothic elegance, he wore nothing but understated designer looks, and everything about him oozed polish and class.

I flipped through the glossy trifold brochure for Bulbrook Grove. For the umpteenth time, I marveled at the gorgeous photographs of stunning forest views, mouthwatering meals, and high-end furnishings. Giddy excitement bubbled up inside me and I craned to catch a view of Bulbrook Grove, the beautiful old pile, in case it popped up over the next hill.

"If this place is half as amazing as their brochure makes it look, I'm sure we're going to have an unforgettable weekend." I spun in my seat, but instead of sharing my excitement, my vampire boyfriend wrung his big hands. I took in the worried pinch of his thick brows and shot him a sympathetic look.

"The tearoom's going to be fine while we're gone."

"Or you'll come back to a new water feature."

I shot Gus a flat look, but he smirked and kept his eyes on the gently winding dirt road.

I turned back to Fitz, who nodded and pressed his dark eyes shut. "I know, I know. The plumbing is in the hands of the professionals, but I can't help but feel I should be there to supervise." He let out a pensive sigh, and my stomach twisted with sympathy.

When the manager of Bulbrook Grove had reached out with a promotional opportunity, we'd taken it as a sign. The brand-new wellness resort in the countryside outside Bath had recently finished renovations and planned to offer guests a Jane Austen Wellness Retreat. They'd learned about our Jane Austen-themed tearoom and offered a comped room in exchange for promoting it to our diners.

Bath was a big draw for Austen fans (like me), as the writer had lived there for a time and set some of her books in the lovely city. Since Roman times, the city had also been a spa town, drawing travelers to its healing waters—the very ones I drew my magical powers from. A wellness retreat with Austen themes seemed a perfect fit for both our regulars and out-of-town guests.

So long as we enjoyed our experience, of course.

I was dying to go, but it took a little more convincing to get Fitz on board. The vampire did all the baking for the tearoom, and it really couldn't function without him. So, I suggested taking the opportunity to get out of town and close the tearoom for a long weekend. Which would also give us the chance to get some long-needed repairs done on the cafe's practically ancient plumbing.

Fitz, who still dressed and spoke like it was 1809, had a difficult time with change, so I knew being away from his beloved Bath Butler Cafe wouldn't be easy for him. Hopefully, Bulbrook Grove's relaxing services would make it easier.

We trundled along at a careful pace over the uneven road. We hadn't passed a home, village, or building for miles, so it stuck out when we drove by a big wooden sign announcing the next turn-off for Feldman Farms. Unfortunately for the farm, a big foreclosure notice was tacked to the sign.

"Florence, the manager, mentioned we'd pass a farm and then Bulbrook would be the next stop."

We climbed a small hill, and at the top, the stunning manor house came into view.

"Wow," I breathed.

"Indeed." Fitz leaned forward, ducking his tall frame to glance up at it through the windshield.

Fitz had lived his prime years during the Regency before being turned into a vampire, and clung to the familiar. I hoped the manor house would feel a bit like home to him. In fact, his own estate had probably looked much like

Bulbrook in its prime, but in the hundreds of years since had fallen into disrepair. Fitz was saving up proceeds from the tearoom and his recently reopened hedge maze to fix it up.

I quirked a brow. "Maybe Bulbrook will give us some ideas for fixing up your place."

His dark eyes sparkled. "Perhaps."

Soon we parked on the expansive white gravel drive in front of the beautiful house, and Fitz grabbed our luggage. There were only a few other cars parked, and none I recognized.

I raised my brows at Fitz as we crunched up toward the grand entrance. "Guess we beat the guys here."

I'd managed to finagle comped rooms for the handsome butlers who staffed Fitz's tearoom. As marketing manager, I explained that our guys had their own fan bases and that if they could speak about Bulbrook Grove from their own experience, it'd be much more likely to sway our customers to give the place a chance.

Fitz grinned down at me. "You certainly worked your magic to make sure everyone got to experience this."

I beamed and lowered my voice. "And I didn't even have to do any real magic, either." I twiddled my fingers as if casting a spell, then frowned at Gus.

"Are you looking for someone?"

"No." He immediately stopped swiveling his head right and left, though the slightest pink blush stained his pale cheeks.

Fitz and I exchanged amused looks. What was up with him?

We climbed the long flight of stone steps up to the pillared entrance and stepped through the double height door that'd been propped open with a miniature iron bust of Jane Austen. Cute—I'd have to ask where they got that.

The circular foyer was an imposing sight, with high

molded ceilings, checkered marble floors and a heavy, polished wooden check-in desk topped with a lovely bouquet of fresh garden flowers. We stepped up to the desk but found no one in sight to greet us.

I nibbled my lip and looked down each of the long hallways that stretched away from the parlor. Raised voices echoed from the left, and after a glance at Fitz and Gus, I crept toward the sound. The beige carpet runner kept my steps quiet as I approached an open door.

"Care to explain this charge?"

The woman's voice sounded tense.

A heavy sigh followed.

"You can't sigh off five hundred pounds, Florence!"

The other woman, Florence apparently, clicked her tongue. "Oh, come now, it was only a bit to, you know, grease the wheels."

An angry scoff.

"It's how these things are done," Florence soothed.

Footsteps sounded and I dashed back down the hall before two women emerged from the room. As soon as they saw me, both grew red-faced. Seemed like I'd walked in on something.

The younger blond woman, maybe in her late thirties, straightened her pale blue blazer and plastered on a strained smile. "Oh, hello. Yes, can I help you?"

The other woman, maybe in her late forties, shot the blond a sharp look. "These are obviously guests you should be checking in." She turned to me and huffed her annoyance. "My apologies." She raised her brows at the blond. "Florence?"

"Right this way." Florence hurried forward and gestured at the front desk where Fitz and Gus still stood with our luggage. Her heels clicked on the marble floor of the foyer as she strode behind the desk.

The other woman hovered nearby with her arms

crossed. Based on the way she was directing Florence, I got the impression this woman was her boss, though she wore no makeup, had her dirty blond hair pulled into a messy bun, and her outfit consisted of dirt-covered overalls and flannel. It was quite the contrast to Florence's polished look.

"Welcome to Bulbrook Grove. Apologies for the wait, but we're so glad you're here. I'm assuming you're checking in for our Jane Austen Retreat weekend?" Florence looked from Fitz, to Gus, to me.

My boyfriend nodded and gave her our names.

"Oh." Florence's light blue eyes lit up. "Minnie, we spoke on the phone."

I grinned. "Pleasure to meet you in person."

"Likewise." She gestured at the grumpy woman watching her like a hawk. "Eleanor, these are our special guests from that delightful Austen-themed tearoom, the Bath Butler Cafe." She addressed us. "This is Eleanor Chang, one of Bulbrook's owners."

"Oh." I raised my brows, surprised again at the woman's casual dress for an owner.

"Thank you for having us as guests." Fitz inclined his head and Gus winked.

"Charmed."

She shrugged. "Ellie's fine."

Florence leaned forward over the high counter and lowered her voice conspiratorially. "I can't wait to meet your hunky butlers."

I chuckled. To me, they were just friends, almost like brothers. But I knew a lot of women shared her sentiment. "They should be here soon."

Florence giggled, but stopped short as a man loudly cleared his throat. She looked up and sobered as a stocky guy, probably in his early fifties, approached from the hallway on the right with his arms stretched wide. "Welcome to Bulbrook Grove. I'm the owner, Bobby Chang." He waggled his thick black brows as he smiled so wide that dimples showed in his full cheeks. "Maybe you've heard of me? Famed London chef retired to the pastoral countryside." He chuckled as he strode forward, shoulders squared, and shook each of our hands.

"Co-owner," Ellie chimed in.

Bobby rolled his dark eyes. "Of course! I couldn't neglect to mention my talented wife—you've met Ellie, yes? And our manager, Florence—what would we do without her?"

We all nodded, and I marveled at the energy rolling off this guy. He seemed like the life of the party.

"Are we all checked in?" Bobby rubbed his thick hands and looked to Florence, who nodded the affirmative. "Fantastic!" He glanced at his wife. "Ellie, could you show our guests to their rooms?"

She started to protest, but Bobby cut her off and motioned at Florence to follow him. "I need a quick word with Florence."

"Of course." The manager's cheeks flushed pink as the two hurried away. Ellie stomped behind the desk and plucked up our key cards and a couple of white packets.

"Follow me, please."

2

SETTLING IN

Ellie showed Gus first to his room, then spun on her heel and briskly led us to ours. I had to nearly jog to keep up as she sped down the high-ceilinged hallway lined with vases of fresh flowers and marble busts. Someone was in a hurry—or maybe resented having to do Florence's job.

Ellie swiped the key card and pushed open the paneled door into a lavish suite. I barely had time to admire it before she handed us the packets and launched into her spiel.

"Welcome drinks and tour are at three; we'll leave from the lounge. Inside your packet you'll find the weekend's itinerary, a map of the manor, and general information about Bulbrook Grove." She spoke quietly, but clipped, and promptly left us to explore the room on our own.

Once the door clicked shut behind her, I turned to Fitz. "Wow. This place is... wow." After the odd welcome, my giddy excitement returned as I practically skipped around the suite. Plush wingback chairs, tasteful furniture, and floor-to-ceiling paned windows that offered breathtaking views of nothing but endless green woodland and meadows. It made me want to frolic in the fields with my beloved copy of Jane Austen's complete works clasped to my chest, and live out my well-read princess fantasy.

I peeked into the en suite bathroom with its freestanding soaking tub, marble countertop, and glittering chandelier dangling from the ceiling. "Ah! I can't wait to have a bath!"

I spun and kneeled on the window seat, gazing down at the pristine lawn below that sloped down to a ribbon of sparkling water—the river that cut through the property. Bordering the lawn to the left stood a lush garden, and to the right a tidy tin-roofed stable and connected garage.

I didn't spare them much of a look, though, before my eye was dragged up and outward again to the vast expanse of verdant nature. Birds chirped outside the window, and the entire place exuded a restful and fresh ambience.

I took a deep breath and chuckled as Fitz came to stand beside me. "Aside from the faint whiff of fresh paint, this place is absolutely perfect."

He tipped his head to the side. "Faint for you, perhaps."

True—with his supernatural senses it probably smelled quite a bit stronger to him. I turned and took in the room. "This is the nicest place I've ever stayed."

Fitz hovered near the window. "I'm honored to share it with you."

Something about his more formal tone made another aspect of the room come into focus—the enormous king-sized bed that took up the majority of the room. Ice flooded my stomach, and I shifted on my feet, suddenly nervous. Oh, right. That thing I'd been fretting about but decided to push to the back of my mind came rushing back to the forefront. This would be our first night alone together, sleeping in the same bed.

I gulped, my throat suddenly dry. Sure, Fitz had fallen asleep on the couch with me at Gus's a handful of times, but he'd never spent the night up in my attic room. It was too awkward with Gus liable to come home anytime. With his superior hearing, there really wasn't any privacy there. And Fitz's derelict place was out until he got it renovated.

Plus, with my vampire boyfriend's old-fashioned manners and sense of propriety, I didn't know quite where he stood on the whole intimacy thing. So instead of talking to him about it like an adult, I'd avoided the issue as a problem for future Minnie to figure out. Well, the future was now, and the bed suddenly felt like the proverbial elephant in the room.

"Uh..." I cast about for anything to talk about that didn't involve sharing the room together for the first time. "I better check on Tilda." Mim, my witchy mentor, had agreed to watch my cat for the long weekend. Besides me, she was the only witch who could telepathically speak with my familiar, and Mim treated Tilda like a precious baby. There was no one I'd trust more to look after her, but still, acting like a helicopter fur-mom provided a convenient excuse to avoid any potential awkwardness a little longer.

"Oh, yes, of course." Fitz sounded almost as relieved as I was to not have to have "the talk." "I'll unpack."

"Oh, good idea."

He eagerly dug into his luggage—a leather train case and a literal steamer trunk (apparently he hadn't purchased suitcases since the 1800s)—as I got comfy in the window seat and made a video call. After a couple of rings, Mim picked up. She smiled at me through the camera, her blue eyes twinkling, the low beams of her cottage store behind her dripping with dried herbs and flowers.

"Hello, pet! How is the place?"

I smiled back. "Good, good. We just got checked in, and I can't wait to explore. It's gorgeous. First, I wanted to check in on Tilda, though. How's my little gal doing?"

"One moment, poppet." The camera blurred with motion as she bent and scooped up my little black cat. "Say hello to your witch mummy."

Tilda narrowed her bright yellow eyes. *You abandoned me.*

I blinked, surprised to find our telepathic communication worked through the phone.

She hissed, and I shot her an arch look. "Hardly. Mim's going to spoil you rotten. And I'll miss you, of course, but they have a strict no-pets rule here."

She flattened her ears as Mim adjusted the phone to give me a better view of Tilda. *I'm not a pet, I'm a familiar. Did you even try to explain that to them? What will you do without me when you get into trouble, hm?*

I scoffed. "*When* I get into trouble? Come on, Tilda, I'm sure I can avoid a magical emergency during a retreat weekend—it's all about relaxing and chilling out."

Tilda sniffed. *Doubtful. You're always getting into trouble.*

I gawked and looked to Mim for support, but my mentor sucked on her lips and looked away. I saw how it was.

"Look, I should go. We have orientation soon. But I'll check in again later. You be good for Auntie Mim, okay?"

Tilda's tail angrily swished behind her. *Maybe I'll stay with Mim and become her familiar and then you'll be sorry.*

Mim mouthed, "It'll be fine."

I gave her a little wave, then bid them both goodbye and hung up. I looked over at Fitz, who was hanging one of his white button-ups in the wardrobe. "Did you catch that? Tilda's giving me all kinds of grief."

He grinned. "I'd expect no less. I suppose you shall have to win her over with extra tuna when we return."

"I think you're right." Movement outside the window caught my eye, and I glanced down at an old lady with white hair meandering across the lawn with her hands clasped behind her back. "I think I've spotted another guest."

Although Fitz, the butlers, and I, as well as Gus, took up much of the space for the weekend, Florence had informed me they'd have some other comped guests staying here, as well.

"I wonder who they'll be," I mused. Florence had told me this was something of a soft launch for the retreat center. They'd invited others who, like us, could help promote the place. As marketing manager for the tearoom, I was curious about potentially meeting other local business owners we might be able to partner with.

The older lady seemed to be exploring the grounds and eventually wandered into the stables. I opened the white glossy packet Ellie had given us and pulled out the map of the estate, plus the itinerary and a list of various classes and services we could choose from.

"Looks like there's a class about taking care of homestead animals—I wonder if that includes the horses."

I glanced over to the stable again as the older woman reemerged, red-faced, arms pumping, and marched back toward the manor house with her back straight as a rod. I frowned and shifted in my seat to get a better view of everything down below. What had her practically fleeing the stable like that? A moment later, Florence and Bobby crept out of the stable.

I sucked in a breath. "Whoa—Fitz." I waved him over to the window as Florence and Bobby, also red-faced, scanned the lawn, then parted ways. Bobby's thick crop of black hair looked mussed, and Florence adjusted her rumpled blazer.

I flashed my eyes at my boyfriend. "I think the old lady might have interrupted those two *together* in the stable."

Fitz frowned deeply. "They certainly appear flummoxed."

My first thought was the old woman had caught them getting up to something romantic, but would they really do that right under Ellie's nose? If not that, then what?

I turned my back to the window and tried to put it out of my mind. I was not going to let my imagination and sense of curiosity run amuck and prove Tilda right. I was determined to stay out of trouble this weekend.

For the next little while I perused the materials Ellie had given us, then unpacked, and Fitz and I took turns freshening up in the bathroom.

He checked his gold pocket watch. "It's nearly three."

I nodded and moved to the door to slip back into my booties. "Time for the welcome drinks."

We stepped into the hall, made sure the door was locked behind us, then froze.

"Hey, Minnie."

My mouth fell open. "Kurt?"

Fitz shot me a wide-eyed look full of fear, which I returned.

I stayed rooted in place as the tall man stomped toward us in his characteristic trench coat and tall combat boots. "What are you doing here?"

He seemed a bit surprised at my tone. He smirked. "You made the weekend sound so unmissable, I decided to book a room myself."

I shook my head. No. No, this couldn't be happening. He was staying here? The entire weekend? Nothing about this man, a rough around the edges vampire hunter, seemed congruent with a luxury spa retreat weekend.

He turned to Fitz. "Kurt Alpenjager. Pleased to meet you." He shook my boyfriend's hand as Fitz mumbled, "Fitzgerald Connors."

Kurt frowned down at their hands. "Chilly."

Oh no, he'd noticed Fitz's cold touch, typical of vampires. "You can't be here." Maybe it was rude, but I didn't care. "This is for industry professionals."

My chest grew tight with fear for myself, my vampire boyfriend, and all my supernatural friends and butlers. What if this man, who was trained to sniff out and kill vampires, discovered our true natures and hunted *us*? It'd certainly be a lot easier for him with us all sharing a manor house for a three-night retreat. This was an unmitigated disaster, and he needed to leave now.

"Well, I may have fudged my credentials a bit." He winked. "But in truth, I may have more industry connections than you might guess."

Like that wasn't mysterious. What was he talking about? And what made him want to join so badly?

I mentally slapped my forehead. He, DI Prescott, and I were on a text chain, since they were both under the impression that I, too, was a vampire hunter. Pretending to be one was the only way to keep myself and my friends safe, but I avoided those two as much as possible. Still, somehow over the months we'd gone from brief hunting related updates, to Kurt sending us Twilight memes and chatting about weekend plans. For someone who claimed to be a lone wolf, Kurt certainly seemed eager to make friends. Prescott and I were probably the only people he knew here, with the rest of his family and friends back in his hometown in Croatia.

Recently, the two of them had been pressuring me to hunt for vampires with them this weekend, so I'd given them my excuse about staying here at Bulbrook Grove. I'd even talked it up out of excitement. My stomach twisted at the thought that this had convinced Kurt to come stay here. *This* was my fault.

Kurt smiled at Fitz—a smile that didn't quite reach his eyes. "Mind if I have a word with Minnie?"

He didn't wait for a response before clapping me on the shoulder and tugging me down the hall a bit. Of course, he'd have had to go to the far end of the manor before we'd have been out of range of Fitz's supernatural hearing, but he didn't know my boyfriend was a vampire. And I intended to keep it that way.

He bent his tall frame and whispered, "You're not the only reason I'm here."

I raised my brows. "I'm not?"

He shook his head, shot Fitz an overbright smile, then grew grim as he turned back to me and whispered, "Places like these tend to attract vamps."

I shot him a doubtful look. "Luxury spa weekends?"

He nodded. "Oh, yeah. These 'wellness' retreats are kind of like cults. All the guests are really open-minded—a little *too* open-minded and open to alternative means of living... or dying." He raised his brows high. "Vamps like to hunt at these types of places for victims because they're easy to convince, no need for coercion." He pointed two fingers at his eyes, then at mine. "I'm going to be watching, on high alert, for any sign of a vampire presence."

My knees almost buckled. "Oh... good," I squeaked out.

He winked. "No worries, Minnie. I got your back." He fist-bumped my limp hand.

I might be sick. All my hopes and dreams for a peaceful, rejuvenating weekend—maybe even one where Fitz and I took our relationship to the next level—evaporated into a heavy sense of dread.

Kurt lowered his voice. "Oh, say, your friend—the tall blond one—he's not going to be here, is he?"

I didn't even have time to answer before Gus threw open his door and strode out into the hallway in tight black leather pants and a trendy jean jacket. Their eyes met, and they smiled at each other.

I pinched myself, convinced I was having a nightmare. But nope. I didn't wake up, and now my arm stung.

3

WELCOME

I smiled and waved at my friends—Al and his wife Yasmine, a fellow witch; Calvin, our youngest, freckled butler; Leo and Cho, who loved to bash on each other; and finally Dom, who was drawing admiring looks from all the women in the room. A decent crowd—about twenty of us—gathered in a charming lounge area with little groupings of sofas and armchairs that overlooked a sweeping view of the green lawn all the way down to the river.

"Welcome, all, to the grand opening of Bulbrook Grove." Despite his short height, Bobby Chang's effusive energy filled the room. He beamed at us, his full cheeks red, as he stood flanked by Ellie and Florence. If Florence and he really were up to something extramarital, how awkward. We all applauded as Bobby grinned and jokingly took some bows.

He motioned for quiet and continued on with his welcome speech. "Bulbrook has been a labor of love. I've put my blood, sweat, and tears into this place—literally." He winked. "Don't worry, though, none of that is in the food."

I flashed my eyes at Fitz as chuckles filled the room. "I sure hope not."

My vampire boyfriend smirked.

"But I could not have done it alone. You've all met, I'm sure, our manager, Florence Cress, and my wife, Ellie Chang." The ladies each bowed their heads. "And you'll meet the final member of our staff later, during evening yoga. We dearly hope that you find this weekend relaxing, rejuvenating, and above all..." He paused for dramatic effect. "An experience you want to recommend to all your friends, clients, and readership."

He winked, and again polite laughter filled the room.

I grinned—what a showman. I was surprised Bobby didn't already have his own cable cooking show.

"Let's also introduce our esteemed guests to each other. By the end of the weekend, we hope you'll all feel like a big family."

Florence consulted the binder in front of her and gestured to an athletically dressed woman with freckles and curly brown hair pulled into a low ponytail. "This is Olwen Combestock, a mummy blogger who focuses on healthy cooking and nature, with a large following both online and in the local community."

The woman, who looked to be about forty, raised a hand and gave everyone a tentative smile. "Hello. Yes, I'm Olwen, and I'm usually the mummy of the group." She patted the fanny pack slung around her hips. "So if you need a snack, Band-Aid, or wet wipe, you know who to come to."

I grinned, and the group smiled and murmured welcomes.

"Next up," Florence continued as she scanned her binder. "We have Janisa Davies, a popular wellness influencer, and her guest, Karine Morales."

Janisa, the petite blond in leggings, twiddled her fingers in a wave and tossed her ponytail over her shoulder, while Karine gave a huge cheesy grin and waved at everyone. "Just so happy to be here."

Cho nodded at each of them and winked. Oh, brother.

"We're also pleased to welcome Nathan Woods, noted travel writer for the UK's biggest travel magazine, *Journey*, who's doing a piece on domestic wellness retreats. We're very honored to be included."

Nathan, a bald, dark-skinned man with a good-natured smile, waved at everyone. A high-end looking camera hung around his neck. "I've actually recently started my own travel blog, where I'll feature my review of Bulbrook Grove —Nathan's Notes, at Nathansnotes.com. Check it out."

Bobby frowned a bit, and Florence nodded. "Oh, right, good. Um, we've also got Mr. Fitzgerald Connors, his marketing manager, Minnie Wells, and their team of butlers from the Bath Butler Cafe, a local tearoom with a Jane Austen theme." They lumped Gus in with the butlers, as I'd snuck him in by claiming he was also an employee.

Bobby crossed his arms and looked my tall boyfriend up and down, from his coattails to his ascot. "And he'll be our resident Regency scholar by the looks of it."

This drew some grins, but I found Fitz's cold hand and squeezed it. He gave me a grateful squeeze back.

"You know I think you look dashing."

He grinned down at me, a sweet twinkle in his eye.

Florence gestured at Kurt, with his scruffy beard, scars and long trench coat. "We also have Mr. Kurt Alpenjager a um—" she squinted at her notes. "Trauma counselor with his own private practice?"

Seriously. That was his cover? I couldn't have told you what a counselor should look like, but I could confidently say it wasn't Kurt. The hunter winked at me, then nodded at the manager. "My patients could really use a rejuvenating experience like this place."

Florence cleared her throat. "And lastly, we have, uh, Irene Fernsby."

A sour-looking old lady—the one I'd seen wandering

into the stables—shuffled forward and barked out, "I'm a crotchety old lady who has no business being here, but, well... it is what it is."

"Uh," Bobby plastered on a bright grin and rubbed his hands together. "Irene's our guest, and while she lacks industry connections, we're happy to have her join us."

Irene scoffed.

Wow. This lady wasn't kidding when she called herself crotchety.

Bobby splayed his hands. "Now, on to the nitty gritty. While Bulbrook will offer a variety of retreats in the future, you've joined us for our Jane Austen Wellness Weekend. While it might seem like the author could only offer us sage advice when it comes to our love lives, Ms. Austen was actually a writer who analyzed, commented on, and gave advice in all areas of life."

I edged forward, my interest piqued. Austen was, after all, my favorite author, and despite years of reading and rereading her works, this was a fairly new perspective for me.

Bobby splayed his hands. "Within Austen's novels and personal letters, scholars have actually discovered an abundance of wisdom relating to all areas of wellness, from what and when one should eat, to exercise tips and more. And throughout this weekend, we'll be sharing such wisdom with you, with, of course, some modern twists here and there."

I glanced to my left. Kurt and Gus stood close together, exchanging a few words here and there. I stuffed down the nauseating feeling of deep worry twisting my stomach and tried to focus on Bobby's promise of a fascinating and relaxing weekend.

The charismatic owner gave us a sheepish grin. "Plus, it doesn't hurt that half the tourists in Bath are here because of ol' Austen. Let's hope it helps bring in some business, eh?"

There it was. I had a hard time seeing Bobby as a big fan of Austen's, so I suspected he was merely jumping on the theme as a business opportunity. I didn't blame him, but I still hoped for some new insights about my favorite author.

Florence stepped forward, tucking a strand of blond hair behind her ear. "Within your welcome packets, you've all received the weekend's itinerary. During class or service times, you're welcome to choose from a variety of options, though if you're interested in a massage, please be sure to book as early as possible, as slots may fill up."

Bobby nodded and briefly put a hand on the small of Florence's back. Whoa—that was pretty flirty. Fitz confirmed he'd seen it, too, with a raised brow.

"This afternoon, we'll give you a tour of our gorgeous grounds, followed by dinner, our big meal at four. I know it seems early." Bobby chuckled and raised his thick palms as if in surrender. "But we'll explain the very sound logic behind it at the table. At six, we've got a relaxing evening yoga class, followed by supper, a light snack, at seven, and then free time until we all retire to bed." He clapped his hands together and swept his gaze over all of his guests. "Any questions?"

No one spoke, so he grinned. "Delightful. If you have any, direct them to Florence—she knows far more than me."

The blond grinned and playfully swatted his arm, while Ellie stood quite still on Bobby's other side, her expression unreadable.

Awkward.

Bobby squeezed Florence's shoulder. "Should we pass out the drinks?"

"Right." She bustled over to an elegant bar cart laden with trays of champagne flutes filled with bubbly.

Olwen, the mommy blogger, cleared her throat as Florence passed out drinks. "I have a question—Jane Austen approved of alcohol?"

Bobby nodded. "Thank goodness, she did." He chuckled. "The golden rule, right? Everything in moderation."

Beside him, Ellie snorted.

I raised a brow. Maybe Bobby wasn't known for his moderation?

Everyone soon had their glasses, and Bobby raised his own. "Please join me in a toast. To Bulbrook Grove!"

I lifted my flute and joined in the chorus of "to Bulbrook Grove," then took a sip of the sparkling wine.

"Let's all have a look, then, eh?" Bobby waved his arm, gesturing for us to follow, as he led the way with Florence and Ellie trailing.

I slid over and gave my friend Yasmine a hug, then greeted my butler buddies. "Hey, guys."

"Nice digs." Cho waggled his thick brows. "Thanks for getting us rooms. Great views, too." He jerked his chin toward Janisa and Karine in their leggings and workout gear. The blond was posing in front of a grand fireplace, while the brunette snapped a dozen pictures of her on her phone.

I rolled my eyes at him as we all shuffled after our hosts down a long hallway.

Leo rolled his stocky shoulders as he peeked into a doorway that led to a cozy library. "I hope they have an actual gym."

Dom nodded his agreement. Those two had seemed the most excited about the actual wellness aspect of the weekend. I knew Cho was here for any potential single ladies, and Yasmine was still recovering from a magical curse that had left her in a coma for three years. She and her husband Al could use a romantic weekend together. The thought reminded me of the looming question about *if* and *how* Fitz and I would take our relationship to the next level. My gut tightened with nerves.

I glanced behind me at the sound of a heavy sigh. Our youngest butler, Calvin, trailed the rest of us with his head hanging. I dropped back to walk beside him. "Hey, Calvin." I frowned. "Wasn't your girlfriend supposed to come?" The university student had been dating Rachel for over a year at this point, though he was pretty private about it. I'd been looking forward to meeting her.

His expression crumpled as he held back tears. "She couldn't make it," he mumbled. He sniffed and looked away. "I'd appreciate some space on this right now."

Oh no. That did not sound good. Cho spun around and grimaced as he made a gesture that clearly indicated I should drop it. I nodded and bit back the dozens of questions I had for Calvin. Had they broken up? When did this happen? Did he want me to hex her? The last bit was a joke, of course—mostly—but I couldn't help but feel protective of Calvin, like he was a little brother. I hated seeing him hurt. Hopefully, some quiet countryside rejuvenation would help lift his spirits.

"Here's the yoga room, where you'll have your session in a few hours." Bobby gestured through an open double doorway to our left. I peeked into a gorgeous room with plastered walls and a massive fireplace.

"It's quite the mood with the fire lit at night," Florence gushed.

She and Bobby exchanged significant looks, while Ellie glanced the other way out a big window.

Yikes. Either Ellie was oblivious to their flirting, or she was so desensitized to it by now that she just let it slide. Either way, it was a weird dynamic.

Bobby led the way further down the hall and lifted a finger, his booming voice carrying all the way to me in the back. "Speaking of fires, after dark, Regency people wouldn't have had electric lights. So, once night falls, it's going to be all candles and firelight for us. There are of course light switches in your rooms if needed." He spun to face us and walked backward.

"We're not going to go so far as to take your phones or computers, but we encourage you to minimize the use of electronics tonight. Let your body adjust to the naturally low light and see if you don't sleep better." He winked. "I'll wager you do."

Janisa snorted and tossed her blond ponytail over her shoulder. "I'm all for holistic wellness, but you'll pry my phone out of my cold dead hands."

Karine shrugged and shot us all an apologetic smile. "What would her followers do without her?"

"Perish the thought," I muttered to Fitz, who grinned.

Bobby spun around again and paused in front of two doors. "Men's and women's locker rooms. You'll have direct access to the indoor pool through there."

"It's stunning," Florence added, biting her lip.

"And here..." Bobby stepped into the room at the end of the hall. "Is our full gym and weight room."

Free weights and mirrors lined one wall, with a couple of treadmills, an elliptical, some cable machines and a squat rack scattered throughout. Huge floor-to-ceiling windows let in lots of light and, like most rooms in the manor home, offered striking views of the lush countryside.

Leo pursed his lips and nodded. "Not ideal, but not bad." Dom crossed his beefy arms and grunted his assent.

Leo smirked. "I call dibs on the squat rack in the morning."

Dom narrowed his eyes, and after a brief stare down, Leo shrugged it off. "Or, you know, I can go second. Whatever."

I smirked. Dom was a man of few words, but he got his point across all the same.

Bobby, Ellie, and Florence guided us out onto the manicured lawn, past the stables and a garage with a Land Rover parked inside. Bobby pointed at the sky. "Now, unfortunately, weather reports say we're supposed to get quite the storm this weekend."

Though we had blue skies overhead with a smattering of fluffy clouds—a lovely early spring day—dark clouds lingered far off on the horizon. Indeed, most of our regulars had been abuzz about the massive storm supposedly headed our way, with lots of fretting over the potential for flooding.

Bobby scoffed. "But it's British weather—never really know what we're going to get, so let's all keep our fingers crossed it stays pleasant, because Bulbrook offers a plethora of outdoor activities."

Florence took over. "Our restored manor house sits on over eighty acres of wildwood and meadows, crisscrossed by this meandering offshoot of the Avon."

I grinned at the glittering river behind her. As a witch who drew my powers from those very waters, it wouldn't be a bad thing to be staying so close to them. It'd certainly give my magic a boost, if I decided to use it. Nathan lifted his fancy camera to his face and snapped some pictures of the river and the rolling hills beyond it.

We crossed the lawn, my boots sinking slightly into the soft, springy grass, and headed toward the kitchen garden.

"This is Ellie's domain." Bobby gestured to his wife.

I guess that explained the dirty overalls.

"We'll have a gardening class tomorrow." I had to strain to catch her quiet words. "We grow most of the food you'll be eating right here or forage it from the land." Chickens clucked in a coop behind her, and I suspected we'd be having some farm fresh eggs, too—yum. Janisa tugged Karine by the sleeve and crouched down beside a chicken, pouting and posing for photos that Karine diligently took. Was Karine her photographer or just a helpful friend?

Bobby nodded. "Ellie also leads our foraging nature

walks and can teach you about horses and—what do you call it, dear?"

She pressed her lips together. "Small share homesteading."

Bobby snapped his fingers. "Right."

I sipped from my champagne flute and finished it off as we climbed the stairs back into the manor house. Irene, the old woman, grumbled as we climbed. "How much farther is this tour going to be? If I'd have known it was a marathon, I'd have stayed put inside and had more champagne."

Inside, we headed in the opposite direction of our rooms.

Florence led the way into a grand dining room. "We'll be having our meals here, together, community style." Paned windows lined both walls, and a huge table stretched the length of the room with seating for twenty. At one end sat a large fireplace, and at the other, a wall covered in oil paintings that obscured a door behind it.

"Through there is Bobby's kitchen." Florence shot him a smile. "Now I'm sure you're all dying to take a peek behind the curtain to watch him work his magic, but the kitchen is off-limits to guests aside from any cooking classes or demonstrations."

Bobby nodded. "Per Ms. Austen's time, the kitchen was typically located fairly far from the dining room. When we renovated, we corrected that for our needs, but basically, Miss Austen would not have been grazing the fridge."

This got a grin out of me. It was a pretty silly mental image.

Florence spread her delicate palms. "Of course, if you're hungry, only say the word and we'll whip you up a snack, but we intend for meals to be shared for the most part with friends, old and new, while you're here."

Fitz and I exchanged worried looks. Sounded great, unless one of said "friends" was a vampire hunter.

4

DINNER

"Please, everyone, have a seat and Bobby will soon have your meals out to you."

The tour ended in the dining room, right on time for our early four o'clock dinner. I usually ate my own big meal around seven or eight at night, but I was eager to learn about the reasons behind the timing.

Florence beamed and raised a finger. "Oh, and I'll fetch more champagne."

"Yes, please." Janisa gave an exaggerated flash of her eyes at her friend Karine.

Fitz pulled my chair out for me—always the gentleman—and I settled into the plush seat near the middle of the table. Everyone chose their seats and settled in, while Florence bustled about, refilling champagne flutes. Fitz, of course, didn't drink—we'd brought a supply of meals from the vampire blood bank for him and Gus—so I polished off his glass too.

"This is lovely." I smiled up at Fitz, who sat tall, with his perfect posture, beside me. "Does this remind you of big dinners you had in the Regency?"

He grinned, a faraway look in his dark eyes. "It does,

actually. Nowadays, big dinners seem reserved for holidays, if that. But back in my day, it was common for whole families to dine together multiple times a week. Tables were always filled with lively conversation and laughter."

He blinked and seemed to pull himself back to the present, giving me a tight smile, but I could read the bit of wistful sadness in his expression. That did indeed sound lovely. Most of my meals were rushed events, half the time standing at the kitchen counter, and nearly always alone. It gave me a better appreciation of what he'd built with his tearoom. There, friends gathered for long, leisurely teas. And even those who dined alone enjoyed the company of the others gathered close together in our cozy dining room and our courteous butlers.

Florence soon had the fire crackling in the ornate fireplace, then moved down the table, lighting the tall taper candles in brass holders. Interspersed among the candles sat little vases and antique glass bottles full of wildflowers and roses, no doubt freshly picked from the land around us. Huge windows lined both walls of the long dining room, letting in the soft light of dusk. Soon, once the sun set, the firelight would be necessary to see by.

I plucked up the linen napkin in front of me and placed it on my lap, then looked up and down the table to take stock of my neighbors.

Nathan, the travel writer, sat at the top of the table, nearest the kitchen, snapping pictures of the lovely dining room. "Oh, uh—dinner's included, yes?"

He caught Florence as she lit candles on the console table under the window. "Correct. All meals are included during the retreat."

The guy flashed her a grin. "Glad to hear it. I mean, my readers will be glad to hear it. And, uh, what about those delightful little toiletries in the bathroom, can we take those home? How about the robes?"

Florence frowned and moved closer to speak with him in quieter tones.

Wow. Nathan was really milking what was already a comped stay for him. Fitz and I sat across from Leo and Cho, who'd elbowed each other in a silent fight to get the spot closest to Karine and Janisa. Cho was now putting on his smoothest act as I bit my lip to keep from laughing.

"You ladies do this often?"

Janisa didn't look up from scrolling through her phone —despite Bobby's request that we limit our use of electronics. But Karine gave my friend a quizzical look, tipping her head and sending her dark curls bouncing. "This is the opening weekend, so... no?"

Fitz ducked his chin to hide his smirk.

Cho scoffed and bit his lip in what I imagined he thought was an attractive pose. "Psh, obvs. I meant, the whole wellness retreat thing?"

"Oh, yeah!" The bubbly brunette turned in her seat to more fully face him. "Janisa goes to them all, and I get to tag along." She flashed him a huge grin.

I couldn't help my curiosity. I leaned forward. "Tag along? As in, you're her guest?"

Janisa lifted her blue eyes for the briefest glance at me. "She's my intern." She raised her brows at her friend. "I'm teaching her all the ropes."

Karine nodded eagerly. "I'm learning so much from her."

I felt a hint of mistrust and narrowed my eyes. "Intern? As in... unpaid?"

Janisa frowned at me. "Didn't you hear her? She gets access to all the most exclusive retreats through me. Plus, the exposure to other influencers. Priceless." She went back to scrolling through her phone, and Karine echoed her.

"Priceless."

I frowned. The word "exposure" immediately raised my hackles. Exposure didn't pay the bills, and as a younger person myself, I'd been exploited through my fair share of unpaid internships where I learned the priceless skills of fetching coffee and making copies. I opened my mouth to press the issue, but Cho and Leo flashed their eyes at me. Clearly, I was getting in the way of their game.

I raised my hands in surrender and leaned back in my plush chair as Cho waggled his brows at Karine. "Well, this is my first time... maybe you could show me the ropes?"

"*Us* the ropes," Leo chimed in, leaning around his taller friend. "Which way was the gym again?" He flexed his impressive biceps and pointed right, then left.

I couldn't hold it in anymore. I laughed, then brought my napkin to my mouth, trying to disguise it as a cough. Dom, who towered on my other side, shot me a knowing look, the tiniest hint of a grin tugging at his full lips.

Unfortunately for Cho and Leo, Janisa and Karine's gazes kept drifting across the table to my broad-shouldered friend. Unfortunately for the girls, Dom's brooding, mysterious ways usually meant he kept everyone at arm's length. I'd only recently pushed a little closer to him after a shared ghostly experience.

Janisa batted her lashes at my psychic friend. "So... it's Dom, right?"

He nodded, then turned his attention to me. "Minnie, can you pass the water pitcher?"

I happily complied, catching the daggers Janisa was shooting at me. Her jealousy was totally misplaced. Even if Fitz and I weren't together, I wouldn't have any interest in Dom, ridiculously handsome though he was. He and the other butlers were like brothers to me. Still, I got some petty pleasure out of rankling the influencer a bit. I'd bet she was used to getting whatever she wanted, based on how she bossed Karine around and paid her nothing.

Gus and Kurt were on Dom's other side. I strained to catch bits of their conversation, gritting my jaw through my anxiety that they'd sat next to each other. Those two were altogether too friendly for my taste. Friendly led to letting one's guard down, which could easily lead to letting it slip that one was a vampire. Although Gus was my bestie, and I'd even come to enjoy Kurt's oddball, intense personality individually—the two of them together? The pit in my stomach told me it spelled disaster.

Within half an hour of sitting down, Ellie swept out of the kitchen, her arms laden with steaming entrees on white dishes. "Dinner's served," she chimed, the most chipper I'd heard her yet.

Florence stepped away from her conversation with Nathan and rushed over, arms outstretched. "Here, let me have those. I should be doing the serving."

Ellie gave her a tight smile and brushed past her. "No, thank you. I've got it."

"Nonsense." Florence, her heels clicking along the parquet floor, bustled around the dividing wall toward the kitchen. "I can help carry plates out."

"Florence!" Ellie's sharp tone brought Florence and the conversations around the table to a halt. "I insist—have a seat." She jerked her head toward the table. Ellie seemed to grow aware of the awkward silence and attempted to rearrange her features into a more pleasant expression, though the tension remained around her eyes. "You've done plenty today. Allow me."

The blond gulped, her eyes wide, then nodded and wordlessly made her way down the table to an empty seat all the way at the end next to the crackling fireplace. I flashed my eyes at Fitz. This was awkward. Was Ellie a control freak, or had she noticed the overly friendly vibe between Florence and her husband and wanted to keep the blond out of the kitchen with him?

Ellie moved down the table, setting dishes in front of the women first. She smelled vaguely of fertilizer and garden earth as she leaned around me and set down a beautiful plate of chicken and mushrooms with baked heirloom carrots. "We've decided the staff will eat with our guests here," she explained as she moved over to Janisa, Karine, and Olwen. "To foster a more communal atmosphere."

Fitz nodded. "Not very Regency of them, the staff dining with us, but I think it a welcome change."

I grinned at him. I'd had to work with my old-fashioned boyfriend on some outdated views about women and what we were capable of, but elitism had never been an issue for him. He'd always treated his staff like family, and we'd become even tighter knit after all coming out to each other for our magical abilities.

Ellie made another trip to the kitchen and finished setting out meals for the women—Florence, Yasmine, and Irene. As soon as we'd been seated, the grumpy older lady had complained that dinner wasn't ready yet and that she was famished. I knew it was a stereotype that the elderly ate early dinners, but this was ridiculous. I had to wonder when she usually ate, if four o'clock was a late dinner for her.

As Ellie bustled back and forth from the kitchen with more steaming, sumptuous-smelling dishes, Irene harrumphed and rubbed her arms, scowling down the table. A crash sounded from the kitchen, and Ellie jumped. "Uh... I'll be right back."

As she left to check on her husband, Irene loudly grumbled and fussed with her napkin. Florence finally leaned forward and raised a brow. "Yes, Irene? Is there something I can do for you?"

The old lady furrowed her brow and glared at the manager. "Well, for one, you can turn the temperature up in here. For what you're charging customers, you'd think you'd pay the heating bill."

I was impressed with how placid Florence managed to keep her expression. "Apologies." She gave Irene a tightlipped smile as she rose. "Perhaps you'd like to switch places with me? A seat right here next to the fire might do the trick."

Irene snorted. "Just occurred to you, did it? Glad to see you've found your manners."

I raised my brows. Wow. This lady had woken up on the wrong side of the bed. She needed this wellness retreat more than any of us, I'd guess. Still—what in the world was she doing here? She seemed so out of place.

"Wellness? Hmph. Gonna catch my death in here with these drafts!" The older woman grunted as she lurched to her feet, and Fitz, always the gentleman, sprang up and pulled her chair back for her. She shook a finger at him. "Now, this young man knows how to treat a lady."

Florence sucked on her lips, no doubt holding back a retort as they switched places. As Irene settled in beside the fire, Olwen, the mommy blogger, shot her a hard look. She probably wasn't too happy being neighbors with the retreat's resident grump. Hopefully, the warmer spot would appease Irene until she got some food in her. Maybe she simply had a major case of the hangries.

Once Ellie made her final trip from the kitchen, Bobby emerged with his apron still on and a few baskets of dinner rolls in his arms. He beamed at the long table as he passed the baskets to Nathan and Kurt, who handed them down the table.

"This is our first meal at Bulbrook Grove! I hope you all enjoy it." His broad smile and dimples lit up the room. "Jane Austen prescribed a bigger meal earlier in the day—no later than five o'clock—followed by a snack, called supper, a little later on—usually of soup. This meant a long overnight fast until breakfast—which usually took place midmorning, after having taken walks to town or visited neighbors."

Bobby spread his hands. "We'll be taking our mealtime cues from Ms. Austen this weekend, hence our early dinner. And, our beloved author said meals should always be eaten with a healthy amount of good company and lively conversation. So please, join me in raising your glasses to Bulbrook Grove's first communal meal at our opening weekend. May it be a healthful and memorable one."

We lifted our champagne flutes, then dug into our meals.

As I savored bites of juicy, seasoned chicken, creamy fresh mushrooms, and perfectly baked carrots, I couldn't help but agree that Bobby Chang had earned his reputation as a top chef. The simple flavors melted in my mouth and felt tied to the land around us. I couldn't suppress a moan of pleasure when I bit into the freshly baked roll that I'd buttered with a healthy pat. Butter that had apparently come from the dairy cows a few farms over.

Nathan closed his eyes and groaned. "It's all delicious."

Bobby's voice carried over the other conversations, clink of cutlery, and the crackles and pops from the fire.

"Everything's grown and raised locally in our garden, or from neighboring farms. Local, organic, and forming partnerships with our neighbors—that's what we're all about."

A loud scoff drew my attention to the other end of the table, where Olwen grew wide-eyed once everyone's gazes turned to her. She coughed into her napkin and muttered, "Sorry. Down the wrong pipe."

Bobby talked with Nathan about the cooking classes he offered.

"That's great," the writer cut in. "You know, I'm offering an introductory discount for advertisers on my site, Nathansnotes.com. I'd be happy to do some placements for a stay here, but also your cooking classes could attract an audience."

"Er—I'll keep that in mind." Bobby continued on as Kurt and Gus chuckled together over some shared joke—

rankling me to no end. I forced myself to turn away and eavesdrop on the other end of the table.

"Wow. An entrepreneur? Hot."

Janisa preened at the attention from Cho. "Mm-hmm."

Karine pointed at her friend/boss. "And she's launching a new line of wellness teas next month, too." She beamed. "She's such an inspiration. Tell them what they're called."

She nudged Janisa, who flipped her blond ponytail and pursed her lips. "Potentiali-tea." She raised a brow and looked around the table, her eyes lingering on Dom, who continued to eat, oblivious to her attention. "It's a health tea... and it helps you lose weight."

"Get it?" Karine grinned. "Potentiali-tea, like t-e-a? Isn't she clever?"

Though I'd heard weight loss teas were basically laxatives—not good—I chuckled in spite of myself. "That's a good pun."

Janisa gave me a puzzled look. "What's a pun?"

Oh, boy. I considered explaining but waved it off. "Never mind."

"Janisa beat cancer with her all-natural diet and holistic approach to wellness." Karine smiled, all innocent admiration for her friend.

Janisa tapped her temple. "It's all about positive thoughts."

I raised a brow. Was it though?

"Now I'm following her program, and I'm sure it's gonna help me with my thyroid disorder." Karine beamed wider. "I swear, I feel better already."

If Janisa was preaching positive thinking and weight loss teas as a way to beat cancer and other serious health issues, I had major misgivings. But it was Irene who spoke up.

"Cancer, huh?" The old lady, who'd been silently eating up till now, leaned forward, her sharp eyes on Janisa. "What kind?"

The young woman paused, apparently surprised at being addressed by the older lady. Her eyelids fluttered as she flipped her hair. "Lung."

She turned back to Cho and Leo, but Irene poked her fork at the young influencer. "Lung, hm? Who was your doctor?"

Florence sighed and hung her head, picking at the food on her plate.

Janisa's throat bobbed. "Um… he's based out of London."

Irene didn't let up. "Dr. White? Dr. Khatri? Bardeem? What hospital were they out of?" She seemed to know a lot about lung cancer specialists.

"Uh, yeah." Janisa lifted a shoulder. "That one—Bardeem."

"Oh really?" Irene spoke around her mouthful of food. "And what? You're selling this 'treatment plan' of yours to others, now?"

Janisa sat up straighter, prim. "Mm-hmm." She angled herself the other way, as if to end the conversation.

Irene snorted and shook her head as she dug back into her meal with more gusto, grumbling to herself. The rest of the dinner passed pleasantly with delicious food and polite conversations as we all got to know each other, though Irene stayed notably quiet at the end of the table.

Dom and I helped Fitz polish off his food so it wasn't obvious he wasn't eating (he'd drink from the blood supply back in the room, later). I tried to peek around Dom's massive shoulders at Gus. How was he fooling Kurt into thinking he ate human food? Or was the hunter already onto him?

As everyone set their linen napkins on the table and pushed their plates away, Ellie and Bobby rose to clear the table. They quickly returned from the kitchen with a couple of silver trays topped with little glass bowls.

"Dessert is served. Goat milk yogurt with fresh blueberries and honey from the hives down the road, topped with a sprinkle of cinnamon."

Nathan chuckled and leaned back in his chair, pressing his hands to his full stomach. "I think I'll burst if I eat any more." He raised a brow.

I shared the feeling. Still, my mouth watered as I imagined the sweet and tart fresh flavors.

Bobby winked at Nathan as he nevertheless handed him a bowl. "That's the point." The chef moved down the table alongside his wife, handing out yogurts. "In Regency times, dessert was served immediately after dinner—if you were too full, too bad!" He grinned. "This kept them from scarfing down a whole pint of ice cream."

I felt directly targeted by that comment.

5

A STRETCH

I unrolled my black mat on the floor of the pleasantly warm yoga studio. Peaceful, synthesized music filled the air, and a fire crackled in the large fireplace behind our instructor's mat. Al helped Yasmine down onto her own mat beside me.

"Are you feeling up for this?" My friend had been in a curse-induced coma for a couple of years, and it'd left her with some lingering health issues. Some days she needed a wheelchair or cane, but today seemed to be a good day for her.

She flashed me a bright smile, which shone against her tan skin. "Oh, yeah. Besides, restorative yoga's my favorite."

"I haven't done it before." I smiled. "I didn't know you were into yoga."

She nodded as she lay on her back and let out a relaxed sigh. "I used to be—before, you know. Back then, I loved restorative because you basically do some gentle stretches, then get to lay there and take a nap."

Her husband let out a deep chuckle as he winced and groaned, trying to fold himself into a criss-cross sitting position. "Oh good. Maybe I can keep up then."

"You'd think I'd have had my fill of 'napping' by now." Yasmine winked at me. "But those kids have me tuckered out."

She was still volunteering at a local school in Bath, though she'd all but been promised a teaching position starting next school year. They loved her there—who wouldn't?

"I don't know how you do it."

Her eyes widened at something behind me, then Yasmine sucked on her lips as she fought a smile. I turned and followed her gaze as Fitz wandered into the room flanked by Dom and Gus. While Dom's tight athletic shirt strained against his broad chest and Gus's expensive tank and leggings showed off his lean angles, it was undoubtedly Fitz that had caught her eye. I let out a sort of strangled squeak, and my boyfriend's pale cheeks flushed pink when he caught me gawking.

I strained to school my expression as he wove between mats, but I couldn't help being torn between laughing and wanting to give him a hug. I'd never—not once—seen Fitz wearing anything besides coattails, a cravat, dress shirt, breeches, and shined boots or leather brogues. It hadn't occurred to either of us that he might need to trade his Regency wear in for something a little more modern during the retreat, so after dinner Gus and Dom had offered to lend him some workout clothes.

Fitz now stood on the mat I'd laid out for him beside me, self-consciously tugging at the cotton breeches he'd layered over black workout leggings. On top, he sported one of his loose, long-sleeved muslin shirts, undone at the neck to expose a hint of his muscled, hairy chest. He wore one of Gus's performance fleece vests open over it. To top it all off, he sported a terry cloth sweatband across his brow.

Yasmine propped herself up on one elbow, her long

black braid trailing down her back, and gaped at him. "Wow."

His throat bobbed, and he dropped his eyes to the mat below his shockingly bare feet. "Is this for me?"

I nodded, still unable to find the words, as he frowned. "And we sit... on the floor?"

"Nope." Behind him, Irene shuffled into the doorway in sweatpants and a turtleneck. She pawed a hand at us and shook her head. "You-know-where will freeze over before I get down on the ground." She snorted as our instructor, a lithe young woman with lightly tanned skin and a halo of black, frizzy curls hurried toward her.

"Ma'am, we can make accommodations. I have a chair for you, so you don't have to—"

"Bah! Don't bother." Irene waved her off and turned around. "I'll find some more champagne until supper, or whatever nonsense they're calling it."

The yoga teacher frowned after her, then shrugged it off and returned to the front of the room where Karine was snapping pictures of Janisa twisted in various yoga poses.

Fitz lowered himself down onto his mat to my left and scrunched his nose, shifting as if unable to get comfortable. He caught me watching and rolled his shoulders, adjusting the fleece vest. "It's Gus's."

I nodded, fighting a laugh. "And the headband?"

A dark lock of wavy brown hair fell over the terry band across his pale forehead. Fitz lifted his dark eyes to it, then scanned the room. "No one else is wearing these." He whipped his head around to Gus, who sat—to my chagrin— near Kurt at the back of the room. I almost didn't recognize the hunter without his uniform of a trench coat and combat boots. Now he sported dark gray joggers and a tight tank.

My pale blond bestie splayed his hands and mouthed, "Fitz dressed himself."

My boyfriend scowled and ripped the band off his head, stuffing it into the vest pocket. "It's too much."

I reached over and squeezed his cold hand. "You look great. It's just... new to see you dressed this way."

He raised a thick brow. "Good new or please-never-repeat-this new?"

I chuckled. "I think we can work on finding you your own athleisure style." I smiled up at his handsome, blushing face. "But it's kinda fun to see a new side of you."

Our teacher stood and waved for our attention. "Welcome, everyone. I'm Serena, and it'll be my honor to lead you all in a relaxing yoga class this evening." She pressed her palms together and smiled placidly out at our little group, all perched on our mats. Behind Serena, the fire crackled in the massive fireplace, and dusk deepened into night outside the floor-to-ceiling windows with their gorgeous view of the rolling countryside. I could think of worse places to do yoga.

"Let's begin with some heart circles." Our teacher sat criss-cross with her hands on her knees and began to circle her torso. The rest of us followed suit, and Fitz raised a brow as my back loudly cracked. Guess I needed this more than I thought I did.

Candles in tall hurricane glasses flickered around Serena's mat, and as the class continued, the peaceful music, firelight, and gentle stretches had me feeling more limber and open than I'd been in ages.

I had a hard time fully relaxing, though. I kept gazing behind me, checking on Gus and Kurt, who'd placed their mats near each other. I caught them exchanging smiles and whispering something. I leaned close to Fitz as we arched our backs in cobra pose. "What are they talking about?"

He frowned, then followed the tip of my head toward our mutual friend and the vampire hunter. He opened his mouth to reply, but Serena moved closer and pressed a finger to her lips. "Let's let our mind and lips be quiet."

I set my jaw in frustration. What could Gus and Kurt possibly have in common, except that one hunted vampires and the other was one? Not exactly the kind of thing you tended to bond over!

We continued moving through poses that felt wonderful, even as I struggled with mentally staying in the moment.

"Oof." I lifted my head as Nathan, the travel writer, struggled with downward dog, his legs bent and shaking. He winced as Serena moved closer. "I'm a bit tight, it seems."

She smiled and placed her hands on his hips, gently easing him back. "This tends to be a tough spot for all of us. Let your knees bend and heels lift, if needed."

Cho and Leo took immediate note of our teacher's hands-on cues and suddenly were also "struggling." I bit back a grin as I continued to stretch the backs of my legs and Serena approached the now loudly groaning Cho. "Hmm, I'm not sure if I'm doing it right, Serena?"

"Me neither," Leo chimed in, though he and Dom had been chatting earlier about how they regularly mixed yoga into their workout routines. I was sure he was more competent than he was letting on.

Instead of guiding his hips, as I was sure Cho wanted, Serena looked between the two of them, a smile curling her lips. "You know, why don't you two help each other?" She waved Leo over and both men's faces grew stony as Serena showed them how to transition into a child's pose, curled up on the floor, with Leo lying on top of Cho to help his lower back open up. Cho grunted in earnest as the stocky Leo lowered himself down on top of him, back-to-back.

Serena moved closer to slightly reposition Leo, and as she did so he scrunched up his face like he smelled rotten eggs. He shot her a wide-eyed look, which she missed as her attention was on Cho, who was panting for breath. I'd taken some yoga classes in the past where the teachers smelled so strongly of patchouli it made my eyes water. Maybe with Leo's more sensitive shifter senses he couldn't handle her perfume?

Either way, the guys lay there until Serena moved off to help Olwen, at which point Leo rolled off Cho, whose face had turned bright red. I turned my attention back to my own mat, biting back laughter. I didn't know if Serena had caught on to them or happened to thwart their advances by chance, but hopefully that would teach them to hit on the poor lady while she was trying to do her job. They, of all people, should know how annoying that could be. They, at times, had to fend off our customers, aged from twenty to eighty-two, who took *too much* of a liking to our handsome butlers.

Before I knew it, our instructor guided us into our final pose.

"Laying on our backs, our palms raised to the sky or resting gently on our stomachs, let's take a deep breath in through our nose... then out through our mouth." Serena paced between our mats, carrying a candle. "Let your mind clear."

While my muscles cooperated, my mind refused to clear. *How are the plumbing renovations going at the tearoom? What soup are we going to eat for supper? Is Tilda behaving for Mim? Will she sulk when I pick her up in a few days?*

Serena's soothing voice floated over the background music. "Let the thoughts come and go."

Easy for her to say. I peeled an eye open and peeked at Fitz, then Yasmine on either side of me. Both wore serene expressions, their chests slowly rising and falling. Our teacher caught me struggling.

She gave me a small smile and moved closer, weaving

gracefully between everyone reposing on their mats. "If thoughts are intruding..."

Mine were banging down the door with a battering ram.

"...try naming them. For instance, say in your mind, 'thought' or 'feeling.'"

I closed my eyes. Interesting approach. Oops—*thought*.

"Your mind is built to think. Meditation isn't about making your mind stop, but about focusing it keenly on the present to keep you in the moment, in flow."

Hmm. That put it in a different perspective for me. I did that all the time when I cast a spell or scried. Not that it made it easier, but it seemed more familiar. I breathed. I noticed my chest rise and fall and sensed the warm breath flowing from my nostrils across my upper lip. I paid attention to the tingling in my fingertips and the—

A cold hand curled gently around my wrist, and I opened my eyes, surprised at how Zen I'd gotten. I turned my head and shot Fitz a quizzical glance—why did he interrupt my meditation? He flashed his eyes, then jerked his head at our teacher. Serena was spinning, her brow furrowed at all the candles and the fire in the fireplace. The flames flickered and pulsed rhythmically. I gasped—wait, was I doing that?

I mentally shook myself, and the firelight returned to a normal, gentler glow. Yeesh. Good to know for the future that I had to watch my powers when I was meditating.

After a few more moments, Serena gently guided us back to fully conscious, up to sitting, and then ended class with a bow.

"*Namaste*. Thank you all for being present with me this evening." She smiled out at us. "I'll be leading more yoga classes this weekend, along with some water fitness and nutrition classes. Feel free to come to me with any questions. Until next time."

I joined in the chorus of "thank you" as everyone rubbed

their eyes, yawned, and climbed to their feet. Yasmine elbowed me, grinning. "*You're* supposed to be the water witch, and *I'm* the fire one." As I drew my powers from the waters of Bath, Yasmine similarly channeled her magic from fire.

I choked and whispered, "You noticed too?" I grimaced around the room at Nathan, Janisa, Karine, and Olwen. "I hope no one else picked up on my powers going awry." The pulsing, flashing candlelight would've been hard to miss if their eyes were open.

Serena looked directly at me, her brow slightly furrowed, and for a moment I worried she'd heard me. But no—there was no way. She was all the way across the room, which was now loud with chatter and the rolling up of mats.

Yasmine chuckled and drew my attention away from our teacher. She wiggled her fingers. "*My* witchy senses were tingling, but don't worry, I don't think anyone else noticed."

I glanced back at the vampire hunter, my stomach heavy with dread. I sure hoped not.

6

AN EARLY EVENING

After class, Fitz and I split off for a quick change before supper.

"Hey—wait up."

We slowed our steps as Leo, our lion shifter friend, jogged to catch up. With a furtive glance at the others filtering out of the yoga room, he lowered his voice and pressed in close. "Heads up—Serena's a vampire."

I blinked in surprise and turned to Fitz. "Did you know?"

He shook his head. "I didn't recognize her. Perhaps Gus did."

Leo tapped the side of his prominent nose. "I could smell her."

That explained his reaction when she'd moved close to him during class. Leo had sniffed Fitz out, too, with his enhanced senses.

"Thank you." Fitz gave him a solemn nod. "We'll keep an eye on that."

Leo nodded, clapped Fitz on the shoulder, then turned and headed in the opposite direction down the hall toward his room.

I bit my lip as Fitz fussed with the key card, finally managing to unlock our room. "What's wrong with using a regular key?" he grumbled to himself. He was making some modern strides—hotel key cards were apparently not one of them.

I stood in front of the bathroom mirror, fixing my hair and freshening up. "I wonder if Bobby and Ellie know about Serena."

"I doubt it." Fitz called from around the corner. "'Vampire' isn't the sort of thing one typically puts down on a résumé."

I chuckled as I imagined Serena's special skills section—"turning into a bat and flapping away into the night."

I finished up, and Fitz and I had just stepped out the door to rejoin the others in the dining hall when my phone buzzed.

I checked the caller ID. "It's Mim—probably something about Tilda."

"Of course." Fitz nodded at me to take the call and moved to head back inside the room, but I waved him on.

"You go ahead—I'll only be a minute."

"I'll give you some privacy then." Fitz bowed his head, gave me a quick kiss on the cheek, and then strode down the hall.

I pressed a hand to where he'd kissed me, my skin still tingling, and answered the call. "Hi, Mim." The door swung shut behind me as I perched on the edge of the bed.

"Hi, pet. Listen, sorry to bother you, but Tilda insists you packed her tuna and salmon cans, and I'm only seeing salmon."

I guided Mim to where I'd stashed more of Tilda's food while my picky familiar grumbled in the background.

I'm hungry. Why did you hide my food?

After we sorted that out, Mim assured me everything was in hand, and I bid her and Tilda goodbye and headed to supper. Halfway down the long hall, raised voices caught my attention, and I slowed my steps.

I crept forward, listening hard, until I came to the room with all the commotion. I hovered outside the door as Irene's muffled voice floated out.

"You're a fraud!"

Whoa. That was a strong accusation. Whose room was this?

"You need to come clean or—"

"Psht. Or what, lady? You'll write a strongly worded letter?"

I frowned and turned my ear to hear better. That'd sounded like Janisa... or maybe Olwen?

"Hmph! How dare you, young lady. You're going to get innocent people killed! You come clean, or mark my words, I'll do it for you."

I raised my brows in surprise, and heavy footsteps stomped toward me. I barely had time to jump back from the door before Irene stomped out, letting it slam shut behind her. Red-faced, her pale eyes widened as she noticed me and we stared at each other. My heart pounded, and my face grew hot at the embarrassment of being caught eavesdropping. At the same time, she'd been shouting—it was hard not to overhear.

Irene sized me up, then waved a hand. "Eh. Tell 'em I'm not coming to supper."

I raised my brows, surprised. "Why not?"

"I've lost my appetite." She winced a little, pressed a hand to her stomach, then shuffled off down the hall before disappearing into her room, several doors down.

"Come on, we're late."

Karine's voice on the other side of the door startled me, and I sped down the hall, only glancing back when I reached the corner. I caught Janisa and Karine emerging from their room, but before they saw me, I dashed forward and hightailed it down the beige, carpeted runner to the dining room. I gave Fitz a quick smile and took my seat beside him, my mind racing.

Irene had called Janisa a fraud. But why? At dinner, she'd asked a lot of questions about Janisa's lung cancer and the influencer's all-natural protocol for beating it. It seemed Irene thought Janisa was making false claims. Janisa *had* said that positive thinking and weight loss teas were a panacea, so the older lady had a point. But still—was that enough to cause her to shout at the young woman?

Fitz shot me a quizzical look, and I leaned close. "I'll fill you in later."

His heavy brow furrowed with concern. "Is Tilda alright?"

I smiled, grateful that he'd be so worried about my cat. "She's fine—tuna emergency." Janisa and Karine entered and took their seats down the table. "I overheard something interesting on my way here."

Fitz pressed his lips together and followed my gaze to the young influencers. He made a thoughtful noise but didn't press me further.

Florence stood at the head of the table and clasped her hands. "Seems we're all here except Irene. I'll go check on her."

I raised my hand. "Actually, I ran into her on the way here."

Janisa and Karine both whipped their heads to look at me. Awkward. They were probably wondering if I'd overheard their spat with the older lady.

"She said she, uh, didn't have an appetite and would skip supper."

Florence actually looked relieved—probably because she wouldn't have to deal with the cranky old lady. "Well then, we'll get the soup on."

Florence, Ellie, and Bobby soon had us served with a

creamy white soup peppered with hunks of bacon—yum—and freshly baked rosemary crackers. Serena now sat in Irene's seat beside the crackling fireplace. Maybe the older lady had found that champagne, as she'd promised, and had herself a liquid supper. Might explain why she thought it a good idea to yell at Janisa for being a fraud, too.

After I ate, I could barely keep my eyes open. Out the tall, uncovered windows, the dark countryside rolled away beneath us, with the lights of Bath twinkling in the distance. Night fell so much earlier out here in the country without all the light pollution. That, plus the firelight and relaxing yoga class, had me yawning, even though it was barely past seven o'clock. All the other guests seemed to share the sentiment.

The chatter around the table grew quiet, and guests began to excuse themselves for bed. Florence reminded us to check our schedules for the next day and the party broke up into small groups. Serena, who'd joined us for supper, huddled together in the corner with Janisa, Karine, Nathan, Yasmine, and of course, Cho, who was no doubt doing his best to get the instructor's number.

I said goodnight to all my friends and shot Gus a warning look as he stood chatting with Kurt, Bobby, and Ellie. My vampire friend needed to be careful around the hunter.

I then headed with Fitz back to our room. As soon as we stepped inside, I froze. Fitz held a candle holder overhead, which cast flickering, soft golden light over the massive bed that took up most of the room. The bed we were maybe sharing... tonight... for the first time ever. I'd thoroughly avoided thinking about it and managed to put it completely out of mind until now.

My mouth dried up, and Fitz seemed to share the same awkward sentiment. "Er... I'll, uh..." He scooted past me and set the candle holder on the dresser.

"Right. Um, we probably need more light." I hurried to the other side of the room, putting the bed between us. "I'll try a spell—it'll be, uh, good practice."

I closed my eyes and willed my heart to beat slower. This was Fitz. The man I hung out with daily in the kitchen, chatting across the kitchen island while he was covered in flour. The boyfriend I'd shared countless cozy nights and harrying adventures with. Why was I suddenly flustered around him?

I shook my hands to ease my nerves, and gulped. Alright, spell time. I used some of Serena's tips, naming my thoughts, until my mind grew more focused, and then imagined heat in my fingertips. After a few moments, the room grew brighter, and I opened my eyes. A dozen candles flared to life, scattered about the room on the night tables, dresser, desk, and shelves. I grinned, and Fitz beamed back at me.

"Well done, Miss Wells."

I dipped into a little curtsy. "Why thank you, Mr. Connors."

The moment of playfulness evaporated as the bed, now cast in the romantic glow of candles, loomed large between us.

Fitz grimaced. "So..." He rubbed the back of his neck. "There are extra blankets in the armoire. Why don't I make myself a little pallet down here on the rug, and you can take the bed?"

He turned and rummaged through the wooden wardrobe. My stomach sank. Fitz was such a gentleman—of course he wouldn't want me to feel uncomfortable or pressured into doing anything I wasn't ready for. I wanted to reassure him it was alright, but the truth was, I felt a bit out of sorts. I wanted him to sleep beside me; it was just so... new.

"Fitz, wait." He turned with a comforter and pillow bundled in his arms and raised a thick brow. I took a deep breath. "Share the bed with me."

He held quite still. "That's not necessary, I'll be quite—"

I shook my head and moved closer. "I want you to, really." I flashed him a nervous smile, my stomach full of butterflies. "I guess I feel flustered all of a sudden."

His face relaxed into relief. "I do, as well. I was afraid to say anything. I didn't want to hurt you, or make you think I don't want to sleep beside you." His dark eyes sparkled. "Truth be told, some long nights, I've thought of little else."

My cheeks flushed hot, and I stepped closer. "Same. What if we both take it slow?" I shrugged and gave him a sheepish grin. "Dip our toes in, so to speak. Maybe we should try sleeping next to each other before we, uh, try anything else?"

He grinned. "I'd like that." He pulled me into a tender hug, resting his chin on top of my head. I squeezed him back, then pulled away. "I'm going to put on my pajamas and brush my teeth—meet you back here."

We parted, and after I got myself ready for bed, I returned to the room in a cotton set with shorts and a button-up top. Fitz had gone another route. I covered my mouth to hide my smile, but of course he caught it and planted his hands on his hips. "Now what?"

I fought not to laugh. "Your pajamas are, um, more Ebenezer Scrooge-ish than I'd imagined."

My tall, broad-shouldered hunk of a vampire stood before me in an ankle-length muslin nightshirt, complete with a tasseled sleep cap atop his head. He shot me a stern look as I sucked on my lips to keep from laughing, until finally, his handsome face broke into a grin. "Okay, maybe it's time I updated my fashion a bit."

"Nah, I like it." I sidled up to him and wrapped my arms around him in a hug, only to realize with a start that he wasn't wearing anything underneath it. I stepped back and cleared my throat, suddenly feeling flushed. Maybe men's nightgowns were sexier than I'd given him credit for.

We both climbed into bed, and I groaned as I snuggled into the plush mattress. "Oh my gosh, are these like ten thousand thread count sheets, or what?"

Fitz lay on his side facing me, the sleep cap draped over his shoulder. He squeezed his eyes shut and let out a contented sigh. "I think they might be made of clouds."

Maybe it was the bed, and maybe it was the company, but I hadn't felt this relaxed and safe for... well, for as long as I could remember. We lay on our sides, facing each other, chatting until the candles burned low, and eventually I must've drifted to sleep.

∼

I BLINKED—HOW much time had passed? I scrubbed my face and squinted through the thick darkness. A sliver of light flickered under our door, followed by, snickers, a whispered, "Shh! Someone will hear," and muffled footsteps.

7

A GHOSTLY VISIT

I held still, barely breathing, until the noises and light passed, then reached over and rocked Fitz's firm shoulder.

"Huh?" The vampire started awake and shook himself as I magically lit the candle on the table beside me. He yawned and blinked. "My goodness, it's been centuries since I've slept so deeply."

Aw, that was kind of cute. But for now, I was in investigative mode. I jerked my head toward the door. "I heard voices and footsteps."

He scrubbed his sleep-lined face. "Maybe someone had to use the restroom?"

I slid into my slippers and pulled on the plush robe the retreat had provided. "Everyone has their own en suite bathrooms. I'm going to check it out."

In a flash, my sleepy boyfriend was on his feet, tying his own robe around his waist. "I'll escort you."

I nodded my thanks and then slowly pulled the door open. We peeked up and down the empty hall. A golden light shone from under the door of a room down the hall and across from ours. We exchanged significant looks, then crept into the hall.

While the old wooden floor quietly creaked under my steps, Fitz moved with absolute stealth, a shadow floating down the hall. Huh. Vampires would make pretty good spies... or ninjas.

We crept up to the door and held still, listening. I wasn't sure who was staying in this room, but several voices floated out to us.

"Mm, this isn't bad."

I gawked at Fitz and mouthed, "Cho?"

He nodded, eyes wide.

"Right?" Our yoga instructor's soothing voice followed. "And it's super good for you. I guarantee you'll be feeling healthier immediately."

"You know, we could totally do a collaboration."

That was Janisa.

"You know, I probably shouldn't tell you about this but..."

"Ooh, tell!" Karine gushed.

Fitz and I crowded closer to the door as Serena lowered her voice. "Bulbrook Grove is great, but if you want a really immersive experience..."

I edged closer and a floorboard creaked loudly under my foot. I winced and froze.

"What was that?" Karine squeaked. "Did you hear it?"

Footsteps sounded—someone approaching the door.

Fitz swept me into his arms, picking me up like I weighed nothing, and sped down the hall, the walls passing by in a blur. In a flash, we were back inside our room, the door closed behind us, listening hard.

"Did they see us?" I whispered.

Fitz shook his head. "I don't think so."

"All thanks to you," I grinned.

After a few moments of listening intently, Fitz nodded. "They went back inside."

"Late night secret parties?" I raised my brows as we

climbed back into bed. "Who knew a wellness retreat would be so mysterious."

⁓

T*ap tap tap*.

I groaned and peeled an eye open, then turned, surprised, to find myself nestled in Fitz's arms, my head resting on his shoulder. Despite my exhaustion, I couldn't help but smile. He stirred and grunted something about, "no, the cranberry scones," before blinking awake.

Tap tap tap.

"Someone's at the door." I swung the sheets off and had barely slid my feet into my slippers when Fitz surprised me with his vampire speed and beat me to the door. He opened it a crack. "Yes?"

"Can I come in?"

Dom strode into the room, his thick hair a mess as if he'd just woken up and his face drained of color. I hurried over to meet him.

"You okay?"

Fitz pulled an armchair over for him. "Have a seat."

The huge guy plopped down into it and wrung his hands, which trembled.

Fitz and I exchanged worried looks, his sleep cap hanging askew, and I perched on the edge of the bed across from our friend. "Dom, what happened?"

His throat bobbed, his gaze far off. "I saw a ghost."

I bit my lip. "Oh no. That must've been frightening." Dom had recently revealed to us all that he could see spirits —and communicate with them. It'd been something he only ever told his abusive father about—a secret he'd hidden for decades. It was an honor that the reserved guy had opened up to us, and I mentally chided myself for not anticipating that this hundreds-of-years-old manor house might have a few spirits lingering about.

Fitz seemed to share my thoughts. "Bound to be a few errant souls in an old pile like this."

He shot Dom a sympathetic look, but our rattled friend shook his head.

His throat bobbed, eyes blazing. "No. I saw that old woman—Irene? She was standing at the end of the bed, said, 'Which way to the exit?' then"—he snapped his fingers—"disappeared." He scrunched up his face. "Well, actually, she complained at me for being a 'useless young man' when I just stared at her in shock, and *then* disappeared."

The gentle whoosh of the river outside filled the stunned silence that followed.

I gaped at Dom. "Does that mean... Irene's dead?"

~

THE THREE OF us stood in our robes, pajamas, and slippers outside Bobby Chang's bedroom door. We knew it was his because of the plaque beside it on the wall that read "Chang Private Quarters." I was sure he didn't want to be disturbed, but we'd knocked on Irene's door and hadn't gotten an answer. We needed Bobby's help to check on her.

When Fitz's knocks didn't produce any results, Dom pushed forward and pounded against the door until a sleepy Bobby yanked it open a crack. "What?" He blinked his glassy eyes and shook himself. "I mean, yes, can I help you?" He peered out at us gathered in the dimly lit hallway with Fitz holding a candelabra over our heads.

"It's Irene." I raised my brows, impatient. "We think something might've happened to her."

The bedsprings creaked, and Bobby shot a furtive glance behind him before slipping out the door, careful to close it immediately. He pulled his own robe tight around him—a worn blue one, not one of the retreat's luxurious white robes—and frowned at each of us. "Why? What happened?"

I glanced at Dom. How were we supposed to explain that he'd seen her ghost?

Fitz stepped in. "We believe we might have heard a disturbance in her room, but we knocked at her door and were unable to rouse her. We thought it best to notify you."

Bobby scrubbed his face, looking not at all happy about being woken in the wee hours of the morning, but nodded. "Yeah, probably best. Alright."

The tired chef waved us to follow and shuffled down the hall, but we'd only barely passed the next door down when it flew open and Ellie frowned out at us, her hair mussed and glasses perched on the edge of her nose. "What's going on?"

Fitz, Dom, and I exchanged surprised looks. The married couple didn't share a room? If that was the case, who'd been in Bobby's bed? If I had to hazard a guess, I'd have said it was Florence. Suddenly, Bobby's care to make sure we couldn't see past him into the room made sense.

The chef grimaced. "It's nothing—I hope—but we're going to go check on Irene. They think she might need some attention."

Ellie rolled her eyes and muttered, "Shocking," but joined us. "I'm coming, too."

Bobby opened his mouth like he wanted to protest, but pressed his lips together and kept quiet as we hurried down the hall. Once we reached the other wing of the manor home, Bobby's steps faltered.

Ellie again rolled her eyes and pushed to the lead. "You would think an owner would know which rooms their guests were in. Follow me." She knocked at the door and softly called, "Irene? Irene, are you awake?"

We all held still, barely breathing and listening hard.

"I don't hear anything," I whispered. Fitz, who'd obviously be able to detect more with his supernatural hearing, furrowed his brow and shook his head.

"Me, neither. *Nothing.*" He gave me a significant look as he spoke the last word, and chills ran down my spine. Dom turned ever more pale. Fitz would've been able to hear Irene stirring... or breathing. For him to hear *nothing* was a bad sign. I could only hope she wasn't in her room.

Bobby pounded at the door and barked, "Irene! Can you hear us? Let us in!"

Again, no response came.

A door down the hall creaked open, and Karine, Cho, Janisa, and Serena emerged, still in the clothes they'd been wearing yesterday. Had they been partying all night?

"What's going on?" Janisa approached, arms crossed, with the others trailing behind her.

Bobby grumbled, "Oh, great. Now we have an audience."

Ellie nodded. "I'll pop into the office and grab a copy of her key."

Bobby tossed his hands up. "Oh come on, she's an old lady. She probably can't hear a thing, and we'll give her a heart attack by barging in there."

"Well, keep trying then." Ellie flashed her eyes at him. "In the meantime, I'm getting that key."

Cho huddled close to me as he joined our little group. "What's going on?"

I arched a brow at him. "I could ask you the same thing."

It was hard to tell in the dim light, but I was pretty sure his cheeks flushed red.

Bobby kept pounding at the door, louder this time, and called to Irene, but by the time Ellie returned with the key card, there still had been no answer.

Bobby shrugged. "Maybe she went for an early morning walk."

But Ellie shoved right past him, beeped her card against

the lock, and pushed the door open. "Irene? We're coming in."

With the curtains drawn, the room sat in pitch blackness. I shuddered as a chill ran down my spine, a witchy hint that all was not right here. Fitz went still, as did Serena—the vampires detecting something the rest of us hadn't discovered yet. With a creeping sense of dread, I followed Ellie, Bobby, and Dom into the room. Ellie skirted around the bed and threw open the drapes, letting in the gray early morning light.

Fitz followed, holding the candles high overhead to cast the most light. Karine gasped and pointed a trembling finger at the bed.

Irene lay in the fetal position, the sheets twisted in her frozen hands, her eyes wide open but unseeing, and her skin an unusual bright yellow.

Janisa shrieked and covered her mouth, and my own throat grew tight. I looked away from the terrible sight as Dom muttered, "She's dead."

8

UNNATURAL DEATH

An hour later, we all sat scattered around the lounge as the paramedics examined Irene's body. A uniformed officer had shown up, as was expected, but I'd been shocked when DI Prescott arrived—and without his partner, DI O'Brien, on top of it. Bobby seemed surprised, too, as he, Ellie, and Florence gathered next to the crackling fireplace with the detective inspector.

I perched nearby on an old-fashioned sofa beside Fitz and Dom, pretending to fidget with the tie of my robe as I eavesdropped.

Bobby's throat bobbed, his wide eyes fixed on DI Prescott. "Is there something wrong, Detective Inspector?" He wrung his scar-covered, chef-toughened hands.

Prescott's dark eyes flicked from the notes he'd been tapping out on his phone to the man's worried face. "Besides a woman dying in your place of business?"

Florence paled, but Ellie's sharp eyes shone, fixed on the handsome officer's face. "Is that unusual? I mean, not like we expected it or anything, but couldn't she have died of old age?"

Bobby scoffed at his wife. "Of course she died of old

age." He gawked at her. "Why would you even—it was her time, right, Detective?" He frowned when Prescott didn't immediately respond. "I mean... right?" He paled and pressed his hands to his full cheeks. "Oh no, did she not? Is that why *you're* here? I mean, as opposed to the paramedics only?"

Prescott's eyes darted to me, and I quickly looked away, pretending to be fascinated by the terry cloth of my robe. He cleared his throat and addressed Bobby. "Please calm down. We simply need to be thorough. And yes, it's typical to send the paramedics and a uniformed officer or two, but I'm only here because I happened to be free."

Again, our eyes met for a brief moment, and I grew a bit queasy as it occurred to me that I might partly be the reason for Prescott showing up to this fairly routine call.

The detective's throat bobbed. "Excuse me for a moment."

He strode over to our tufted couch near the french doors that overlooked the rolling green valley. It was now nearly seven o'clock, and a rooster crowed from somewhere nearby, but the heavy, dark clouds on the horizon kept the world outside dim and dreary. A heavy mist drifted over the lawn, as if Irene's death had cast a pall over everything, even the weather.

"Minnie, a word?" DI Prescott smiled at me, but his expression grew stony as he nodded an acknowledgment at Fitz.

My stomach tightened with nerves as I rose and followed him out into the empty dining room. Over the past several months, I'd been getting the impression that Prescott may have rekindled some feelings for me that I thought had been put to rest last year. I was with Fitz now, but even if I hadn't been, I wouldn't have returned Prescott's interest. At one point, I'd found the handsome detective appealing, but now he seemed to foster a hatred for vampires that went even beyond that of the hunter he'd teamed up with.

Speaking of whom...

"Wait up!" Kurt jogged over to join us, his signature trench coat flapping behind him to reveal his pajamas. I grinned, both at his outfit and out of relief at not having to have a private talk with Prescott.

The Detective Inspector grunted a greeting of sorts and shot the hunter a dark side eye. I frowned—weird. I was under the impression these two were buddies. Had they had some sort of falling out? Kurt seemed oblivious to any animosity from Prescott, though.

As soon as we'd crossed into the dining room, shutting the heavy wooden door behind us, Kurt, Prescott, and I huddled up. I'd led both men to believe I was a fellow vampire hunter—a precarious lie that I hated having to maintain. But it was the only way to keep an eye on them and keep me and my supernatural friends safe.

Prescott folded his arms and stared Kurt down. "What are you two doing here together?"

Kurt and I exchanged bewildered looks and both hurried to deny it.

"We're not here together." I gestured between us.

Kurt shook his head, scrunching up his face as though the thought of it grossed him out. "No—no way."

I folded my arms. He didn't have to deny it *so* hard.

"Minnie made it sound unmissable." Kurt lowered his voice and twirled a finger. "Besides, retreats like these are usually hotbeds for vampiric activity. I decided at the last minute to join and scope it out." He shrugged. "If I get a rejuvenating weekend while low-key hunting for vamps, all the better."

I shot him a flat look. "Planning to write this off as a business expense?"

Prescott narrowed his eyes, still unconvinced. "Really?

Hotbeds for vampires?" He cast a doubtful look around the elegant dining room.

The hunter nodded slowly. "Oh, yeah. These places attract poor saps looking for some alternative 'cure' or the secret to whole-bodied spiritual wellness, or some other nonsense." He scoffed dismissively. "What better 'secret' could there be than vampire blood? It's a common ploy for vamps to lure these goobers by going, 'Here—try this miracle cure of mine,' of course, not disclosing it contains vampire blood."

I cringed—yuck.

Kurt played the scenario out. "'Now you'll live forever!' Only catch is..." He put his fingers to his teeth and mimicked having fangs.

I laughed. "Are you serious?"

"Oh, dead serious. It's no laughing matter." The hunter stared me down until I raised my palms in surrender.

I could believe vampires lured people to their nest with the promise of health and everlasting life. But targeting yoga retreats? It seemed a little far-fetched to me. Wouldn't it make more sense to find victims in hospitals or doctors' offices, if vampires were pitching a miracle cure? Maybe there was some special need for flexible, zenned out vampires I didn't know about. Prescott finally cracked a little grin, his demeanor softening.

He waved him off. "Alright, alright. I was surprised, that's all." Prescott looked at me from under dark, curly lashes. "Guess I was feeling a little left out and wanted to come see what all the fuss was about when I got the call."

"Oh, heh." My stomach sank. He *was* here because of me. Yikes. I was tired of playing double agent with these two, and now I had to figure out some way to fend off Prescott's advances? All without drawing his attention and anger to Fitz as a rival? Great—easy peasy.

Prescott motioned us closer and dipped his chin. "Now

that I'm here though, I should tell you both, I'm not so sure this was a natural death."

Kurt's eyes lit up. "Do tell."

Prescott bit his full bottom lip. "Was Irene jaundiced like that beforehand?"

We shot him quizzical looks.

"Yellow—was her skin yellow like that? It's caused by jaundice."

I frowned. "No... she wasn't." I'd noticed the odd color of her skin when we'd found her.

Prescott nodded. "And are either of you aware of any health issues she had? Maybe with her liver or pancreas?"

"No, not that she mentioned." I shrugged. "Not that I talked to her a whole bunch, though. You know—she did seem to know a lot about lung cancer?"

Prescott tapped some notes in his phone. "We'll look into it further."

Kurt narrowed his eyes. "What are you driving at?"

The detective pulled his lips to the side. "I'm not sure, yet. It could be nothing suspicious but... I'll get back to you when I know more."

Kurt threw up his hands in exasperation. "Seriously? You can't leave us hanging like that."

Prescott raised a brow. "Think this could have anything to do with a vampire?"

The hunter edged closer, his gaze intense. "Did she have bite wounds on her neck? Any signs of violence?"

"No."

Was that disappointment on the detective's face? Surely, he couldn't be upset that this old woman showed no signs of suffering an attack. "Um, that's good, right?"

Both men turned to me. Kurt nodded, but Prescott frowned deeply. "I'm not convinced a vampire wasn't involved." He pointed at the two of us. "Keep an eye out for any supernatural activity. If one of those creatures is skulking about, preying on the weak, we need to take care of them before they strike again."

I recoiled at the eager glint in his eye and the curl of his lip, like he'd savor the opportunity to kill one of those "creatures." While some vamps were bad news—like Fitz's sire, Darius, for example—others were frankly delightful. I supposed it simply mirrored human nature, but there was no way these two would listen to that.

Kurt crossed his arms. "Well, obviously we'll be on alert, but there doesn't seem to be any evidence to suggest a vampire killed that old lady."

It struck me as odd that Prescott seemed more bloodthirsty to kill a vampire than the man who'd literally been raised to do so. Kurt seemed to view hunting as merely a job that had to be done, while I increasingly had the sense that Prescott relished it.

The detective shrugged. "The coroner will run some tests, and I'll keep you informed. In the meantime, let's get back to it." We followed Prescott back into the lounge as the paramedics wheeled Irene in a body bag out into the foyer.

The detective approached Bobby, Ellie, and Florence. "Will you be continuing this weekend retreat?"

"Uh." Bobby blinked rapidly, clearly distracted and distressed by the body on the stretcher. "Er... I suppose so, yes."

Prescott raised his voice and addressed the whole room. "No one leaves the manor house. I expect everyone to remain here until we give word that you're cleared to go." He turned back to Bobby. "I'll be in touch soon."

The chef gawked as Prescott strode to the door. "Wait! Are we—" He lowered his voice and hissed. "Are we under investigation or something?"

Prescott pressed his lips together and dodged his question. "One last thing—what did Irene eat yesterday?"

Bobby spluttered, but Ellie jumped in to answer. "Irene

had some champagne, we all did, and we ate a large early dinner together of mushroom chicken and carrots. And then—well, she actually skipped supper, so I think that's all she ate."

I stepped forward. "I saw her, right before supper. She said she'd actually lost her appetite." I recalled the way she'd clutched her stomach. "I got the impression she might've had a stomachache."

Bobby gaped at me, then whirled on the detective. "Wait a minute—you think something she ate kil—did this to her?" He gestured around the room, frantic. "Everyone else ate the same dinner; that's impossible. I'm a professional. I wouldn't serve bad food."

Prescott ignored him and turned to me. "She had a stomachache?" He glared at Bobby, Ellie, and Florence. "And no one checked on her?"

Florence, who'd donned another stylish skirt suit, stepped forward. "I did. I called through the door last night, but Irene wouldn't let me in." She shrugged. "She said she was fine and that she just needed to sleep off some indigestion."

Prescott tapped some notes into his phone. "And when you found her this morning, the door was locked?"

Ellie nodded.

"Windows, too?"

"Um... I think so."

He nodded. "Our officer will have checked. Thank you all. As I said, I'll be in touch."

With that, Prescott marched out the door, following the paramedics and Irene's body, and left the rest of us in shocked silence.

9

A HIKE

The wind whipped my hair into my eyes as I trudged across the sweeping meadow. I pulled my hair back in a ponytail, to better take in the breathtaking view. Green hills, lush valleys, and thick forests rolled all the way to the horizon. My heart rose in my chest with a thrilling sensation of openness and freedom. I had the urge to spread my arms wide and frolic through the rustling grasses while singing "the hills are alive."

The only dampeners on my mood were of course, Irene's shocking, sudden death and the dark storm clouds churning in the near distance. Still, I'd file the view away in my memory as one of the most gorgeous of my life. I grinned up at Fitz as we trailed toward the back of the group, a leather bag slung over his shoulder, which held our water bottles and a few snacks. "I'm glad we did this."

He reached over and took my hand. "Me, too."

Our group had debated whether the morning's activities should continue after Irene's death. The impending storm, at first, formed another argument against. But ultimately, Ellie had decided in favor of leading the foraging hike. It was, after all, probably our only chance to experience the stunning nature surrounding Bulbrook Grove before the rain hit for the rest of the weekend.

And Bobby had really turned on the charm, urging us all to go, because "It's what Irene would've wanted." I highly doubted the grumpy older lady would've wanted anything to do with a long hike. Instead, I suspected Bobby was trying to smooth things over, in hopes that Janisa, Olwen, and Nathan would refrain from writing or posting about the death. It had cast a pall over the opening weekend and might give the retreat a bad reputation.

I'd hesitated until Bobby won me over with an argument straight from my favorite writer. "Also, Austen recommended some fresh air and a walk to the next town or to visit friends to work up an appetite before breakfast." I hated to admit it, but thinking back over her novels, all my favorite heroines from Lizzy to Emma were always striding around the countryside in the mornings. I'd come here excited to experience Austen's take on wellness, so in the end, I'd voted in favor of the hike.

As it turned out, the exercise and fresh air seemed to lift everyone's spirits—one more example of Jane Austen's enduring wisdom. We'd all been shaken by poor Irene passing away, but now as we wove our way into the tree line, ducking into the cool shade of the dense forest, the friendly chatter of the previous day resumed.

At the front of our winding line of hikers, Ellie pointed to the right at a tangle of thorny brambles. "Here we have a blackberry bush. Those will ripen later in the summer, and we'll use them to make preserves, pies, and various other delicacies."

All along the way she'd been pointing out edible berries, nuts, birds' eggs, and more. I'd had no idea so much of the natural world around me was edible. I'd been dreading the hiking bit, since I was already tired from a restless night, but it'd turned out to be fun.

Janisa posed beside a tree, stretching her arms to the sky and trying different head angles, while Karine snapped pictures with her phone and cheered her on. "Gorgeous. Yas!"

I picked my way over roots poking through the dark, rich soil. The thick canopy of leaves swayed overhead as birds chirped a happy song all around us. I yawned and marveled at the energy with which Cho, Janisa, and Karine bounded along. We were already an hour into our hike and had been up and down steep hills, but those three practically skipped forward, talking a mile a minute.

I raised a brow at Fitz and muttered, "Maybe we should ask for whatever supplements Serena was handing out last night."

It took a moment for him to recall the after-hours party we'd eavesdropped on, but then he sniffed and arched a brow. "Perhaps." He stretched the word out as if he knew—or suspected—more than he was letting on.

"Cho."

Our friend turned around, thick eyebrows raised, and Fitz motioned for him to join us in the back. He stood aside and let the others pass until he fell into step with us. "What's up, guys? Loving the outdoors? I'm like, I've got to do more camping, this is amazing, right? I mean, right?"

Fitz leveled him a hard look. "What has you so energized this morning?"

Cho scoffed and shrugged. "Er... nothing. I mean, I had a good night."

I raised my brows. "Yeah, seems like you had a *real* good night, considering you were still in yesterday's outfit this morning when we found Irene."

His dark eyes widened, and his cheeks flushed bright pink.

Leo dropped back and gawked at Cho, then narrowed his eyes. "Holy—did you go to an after-hours party and not invite me?" He sported a backpack that also served as a water dispenser, with the drinking tube bobbing on his shoulder.

Cho's blush deepened as he gestured at some random point among the trees. "Hey look, some birds!"

"Nice try. Dude, I thought we were bros."

Cho winced at his friend as Fitz and I trekked along, caught in the middle. "Sorry, but the girls invited me, and you know—girls."

Leo scoffed, his lip curled. "You expect me to believe they wanted *you* all to themselves." He rolled his eyes. "You couldn't swing that."

Cho lifted his chin. "Think whatever you want, I don't care." He stomped off, indignant, and caught up with Janisa and Karine.

Leo shook his head and marched after him, grumbling to himself.

"Those two are too competitive for their own good." I rolled my eyes. "They need girlfriends."

A whimper startled me, and I glanced back at Calvin, who dragged his feet behind us, head hanging. I shot Fitz a worried look. The young, freckled butler was usually the positive, innocent one among us, too fresh to have been beaten down by life. Not that I ever let the blows keep me down, but I had the impression Calvin had never taken any. Until now, maybe.

"Uh... you okay?" He'd been out of sorts yesterday, too.

He sniffled and rubbed his nose, then shrugged. "Yeah."

I gaped at Fitz, then dropped back beside my friend. "Are you crying? Calvin, what's wrong?"

"I'm not crying." He sniffled, and his chin quivered.

He was definitely crying. I shot a helpless look at Fitz, who spread his hands, no doubt feeling as helpless as I did.

"Hey, what's going on?" We slowed our steps, letting

more distance grow between us and the others. "You can tell us."

Calvin shook his head, his gaze far away. "Oh, you know, R-Rachel and I are over." His words grew pinched at the end and he brought a fist to his mouth.

Oh no. No wonder he hadn't wanted to talk about her absence yesterday. And yikes—me saying Cho and Leo needed girlfriends a second ago must've triggered him.

He blinked back tears. "She was the one, you know. I'll never love again."

I bit my lip and slid an arm around his shoulders as we meandered among the quivering trees. "Oh Calvin, I know it feels that way. Believe me, *I know*. You saw me going through my divorce last year—my ex was my college sweetheart, too." I glanced up at Fitz, who walked nearby. I smiled at his broad shoulders and kind heart. "Trust me—you'll find the right girl. Someone who makes you feel a way you never even knew was possible."

A smile tugged at the corner of Fitz's mouth.

It was true, too. As I looked fondly at my boyfriend, I found myself wondering why I'd been flustered last night. I guess part of me feared that taking that last step toward intimacy might ruin the great thing we had going, somehow—like any change at all could throw us off course. I smiled at myself. It didn't make sense and was clearly a baseless fear. In fact, Fitz and I helped each other grow—the changes were part of what made our relationship so great.

But Calvin didn't share my optimism at the moment. He shook his head and let out a shuddering breath. "No—love's just not for me. It's over."

I almost smiled a bit at that. He was what—twenty-two? Calvin had a bright love life ahead of him, I was sure of it. But I also knew what it felt like to be heartbroken and feel hopeless.

I gave his shoulders a squeeze. "Want to talk about what happened?"

His throat bobbed. "She left me for her friend's boyfriend's brother." He whimpered. "They're going on group dates now."

"She chose someone else?" I gaped at him as his face crumpled. "Wait—did she cheat on you?"

He nodded and hot anger flashed through me. "She doesn't deserve you. Do you know how many women would line up outside the tearoom to have a shot with you?"

He dropped his gaze to the leaf strewn path below our feet. "Most of them are like, eighty. Not that there's anything wrong with an older woman, but... that's a big age gap for me."

Our clientele did lean elderly, though there were some college-aged cuties who came in, too.

"It's going to hurt for a bit, but it'll get better, I promise." I thought of Rachel. How dare she hurt our sweet Calvin like this? "Me and Yasmine can brew up a good hex for her—give her one really stinky foot, or curse her to always have a stain on the seat of her pants?"

Calvin snorted, and I counted it as a win to get even a momentary grin out of him. "No. Thanks, though." He let out a sigh that sounded like it came from the depths of his soul. "And then that poor old lady, Irene? I should've been nicer to her, you know? I should've tried to include her more. We all cast her aside and then she died—all alone."

I flashed my eyes at Fitz, who shot back a concerned frown. I hugged Calvin to my side. "You know, buddy, you might be projecting a *teensy* bit. I don't think Irene was overly interested in joining in the group activities. She seemed alright doing her own thing." I recalled the way she'd "noped" on yoga and vowed to go off and drink by herself.

Calvin sniffed, his chin trembling. "I suppose you get

used to being alone at some point." He sucked on his lips and patted my hand.

Oh boy. Fitz grimaced, and I nodded—yeah. This was some serious—and slightly dramatic—heartbreak we were dealing with. At least this was a wellness retreat, designed for healing. What better place for Calvin to be than here, among friends?

Unless, of course, Irene hadn't died of natural causes and we had a killer among us. I shuddered at the thought.

"Everyone gather round!"

We hustled to catch up with the others as Ellie waved us toward her. Once we'd circled up, she crouched down beside a fallen log and pointed into the hollow. Brown mushrooms with small, round caps grew inside in little clumps. "This is an important foraging lesson." She crossed her arms over her propped up knee. "These little guys look innocent enough, right?"

I nodded along with the rest of the group.

"In fact, these are death cap mushrooms."

Yeesh. That name didn't sound good. I shifted on my feet as Ellie continued on, her eyes scanning our group.

"They look a lot like common edible types. You have to be really careful when foraging for mushrooms not to mix them up, as these little guys can cause vomiting, stomach cramps, seizures, coma, jaundice, and even death."

Kurt turned around and caught my eye, mouthing, "Jaundice?"

I sucked in a sharp breath over my teeth. Prescott mentioned that as the reason Irene's skin had turned bright yellow.

Ellie stood and dusted her hands off on her pants. "That's why we're extra careful when foraging. For instance, Bobby uses local mushrooms in preparing the meals at Bulbrook Grove—it's a good thing he's such a highly trained chef, right?"

My stomach sank, and judging by the worried look on Kurt's face, I wasn't the only one. Bobby foraged for our mushrooms? The ones used in the mushroom chicken dinner last night? As in, the last meal Irene ate before she died and turned yellow, a side effect of the very toxic mushrooms growing out here in the forest?

I shuddered and Fitz squeezed my shoulder. "Could Bobby have accidentally cooked poisonous mushrooms and killed Irene?" I hissed. "Could one of us be next?"

My vampire boyfriend gave me a bracing look. "It'll be alright—we'll look into it further."

I nodded as we shuffled forward to continue on our hike. We passed Olwen, the mommy blogger, who crouched down beside the fallen log. At first I thought she was tying her shoelace, but as I glanced back over my shoulder, something else caught my eye. She held a small jar, with something dark inside, then hurriedly shoved it in her fanny pack, before fidgeting with her shoelace and standing.

Our eyes met and hers widened for a fraction of a second before she put on a pleasant smile. "Shoelace." She hustled past me and sped her way toward the front of the line. That was odd. Had Olwen collected a poisonous mushroom?

"Ellie!" Nathan called up to our guide, who spun around. "Weather's turning—maybe we should head back?" He pointed at the sky.

Sure enough, peeking through the dense canopy of the trees, the sky had turned dark and foreboding. As Ellie agreed and retraced her steps to turn us around, Nathan caught up to her. He pulled our guide aside, mumbling, "I'd like to speak with you about something..." I hoped for Ellie's sake he wasn't trying to pitch her advertising spots for his blog, like he had with her husband last night.

10

DIRT

Our group moved straight from the hike directly into Ellie's gardening class, in an attempt to make the most of our outdoor time before the clouds broke. We'd all hustled into the garage next to the stable and thrown gray work smocks over our heads, then slipped on the leather gardening gloves Ellie provided us. It was nearly ten by now—and my grumbling stomach told me it was time to eat. Judging by the looks of the day, though, I wouldn't have guessed the time.

Instead of bright late morning sun, dark, gloomy clouds hung low overhead, and the wind whipped the ends of my ponytail into my face. I knelt between Yasmine and Fitz around a raised planter that burst with rustling leafy greens and little pyramid-shaped trellises wrapped in vines.

Ellie doled out rosemary sprouts for us to transfer to the raised beds, along with little trowels with which to dig.

"Kitchen gardening is a long tradition, and can provide a nourishing and budget-friendly supplement to one's meal planning." Ellie gave a rare, tight smile. "Besides, it can be quite gratifying to grow your own food."

Yasmine took a deep breath and smiled. "Smells like rain

and earth—this is quite fun." She nudged her husband, who knelt beside her. "Hey, that gives me an idea. I should start a garden at the academy; the kids would love it."

He kissed her cheek and spoke in his low, soothing voice. "It's brilliant."

As I dug in the loose, dark earth, I glanced around at my friends, who bordered the planter. "Psst."

Dom and Leo gave me their attention, while Calvin continued to sullenly scrape at the dirt. Cho was in his own world, grinning at Janisa and Karine. Janisa lay on her stomach beside a row of marigolds, pouting, as Karine moved about her, taking pictures at different angles. I rolled my eyes at him and addressed the others.

"Did you guys hear what Ellie said about the poisonous mushrooms on the hike? She said they might cause jaundice, which turns your skin yellow."

Leo's dark eyes widened. "Like, in the way Irene was yellow?"

I held his gaze and slowly nodded. "What if Bobby put poisonous mushrooms in the dinner last night?"

I darted a sly look at Ellie to make sure she didn't overhear me accusing her husband of possibly killing Irene. She stood behind Olwen and Nathan, who worked at another raised planter beside Kurt and Gus. My vampire bestie smirked at the hunter, and my stomach twisted with worry.

"Did anyone else have a stomachache or feel some of the milder symptoms the poisonous mushrooms could cause? Nausea, vomiting?" Fitz, whose sleeves were rolled up to his elbows, addressed the group.

Everyone shook their heads, and I had to admit that Kurt, Olwen, and Nathan all seemed perfectly healthy.

"And everyone made it through the hike, no problem." I narrowed my eyes at Cho. "In fact, Janisa, Karine, and Cho seem positively bounding with energy."

He peeled his gaze away from the girls at the sound of his name. "Huh?"

Yasmine snorted. "Probably because they went to Serena's secret after party and tried her new age supplement."

I gaped at her. "You knew about that too?"

Cho clicked his tongue and flashed his eyes at her. "You're supposed to keep that on the down low! It's not a secret if you tell everyone about it."

Leo shot him a dark look. "You already let it slip, remember? When you let me know that you didn't invite me?"

Cho suddenly grew quite interested in the sprout he was planting.

Yasmine's dark cheeks flushed, and she shrugged. "I got invited but declined." She chuckled. "I'm kind of an old lady now and get way too sleepy for an after-hours party."

"I feel you." She was hardly old, but even I'd been exhausted last night, and I wasn't battling some pretty serious health issues like my friend was. I pressed her for more information, though, as I set some sprouts into the hole I'd dug. "What's this about Serena's health supplement, though?" I scooped loose earth around the exposed roots.

Yas leaned closer and lowered her voice as Ellie paced between the garden rows. "Serena says she's part of some health collective—something outside of the retreat. This place sells this vitamin powder stuff, and she thought I might be interested since my health is obviously, er, less than optimal." She flashed her eyes. "Serena claimed it could cure everything from toenail fungus to broken bones, but I wasn't up for it. To be honest, it sounded kind of like snake oil to me."

I frowned at Cho. "Why be so secretive about it?"

He primly raised his thick brows. "It's very exclusive."

Al chuckled as I rolled my eyes.

Leo scoffed. "Can't be that exclusive if they let you in."

Cho glowered at him.

Nathan, the travel writer, lurched to his feet and dusted the dirt off his gloves. "Excuse me, Ellie?"

She turned and planted her hands on her hips. "How can I help?"

Nathan gave Ellie a sheepish smile. "I hope you don't mind the question—I'm a writer and tend to ask a lot of them."

Ellie nodded for him to continue.

"Uh, those mushrooms you mentioned earlier, the deadly ones... I have to admit they looked very similar to the mushrooms we ate at dinner last night."

So he'd picked up on that, too. At this point everyone, even Janisa and Karine, watched the interaction.

Ellie flashed a rare smile. "You're correct. That's why it's crucial to be knowledgeable when foraging."

"Heh, right." Nathan shifted on his feet, wringing his hands. "Those mushrooms last night, though—you said they were foraged from around here?"

Ellie nodded, a twinkle in her eyes. "Yes. In fact, Bobby gathered them himself." She seemed to register Nathan's pointed tone and hurried to add, "Oh, but there's absolutely nothing to worry about."

He smiled in a way that didn't reach his eyes. "Oh, good."

"Yeah, if there were any kind of mix-up, you'd have already been dead by now." Ellie stared him down for a moment, then moved off, leaving Nathan standing there with the blood drained from his face.

I was sure he was thinking the same thing the rest of us had to be. One of us *was* dead already—Irene. I gawked at my friends, who looked as horrified as I felt.

Leo, wide-eyed, stage whispered, "Did Bobby kill that old lady?"

Yasmine blew out a heavy breath, and Dom raised an alarmed brow.

Calvin finally lifted his head, scandalized. "Wait—like he... *meant* to kill her?"

I shrugged. "Maybe. Or maybe he simply gathered the wrong mushrooms by mistake." My stomach turned. "It could've been any one of us who ate the deadly ones."

Fitz tugged off his glove and put a reassuring hand on my back.

"But like... wouldn't we all have gotten sick?" The mere thought of it had Cho turning a little green.

Leo lifted a palm. "Maybe Irene happened to get a bigger serving of the poisonous 'shrooms?"

"Maybe." Yas made a face. "But if the cafeteria makes something a little off at school, it's never only *one* kid who gets ill. Same here. You'd think *some* of us would be feeling at least a little poorly if we'd had a smaller dose of the death caps, right?"

Beside her, Al's face turned gray, and he leaned back. "Poisoned, at dinner? I've lost my appetite."

"This is serious." His wife grinned. "That never happens."

Leo—always strict about counting his macros and eating healthy—scoffed. "We know."

"I like my food." Al spread his palms.

"Yeah." I shot Leo a teasing look. "Not everyone wants to live off of protein powder."

He lifted his chin. "For your information, I also eat protein *bars*."

This got a rare snort out of Dom.

"All joking aside..." I lowered my voice to a whisper so that the others leaned forward to catch my words over the rush of the wind through the trees. "Does that mean Bobby targeted Irene?"

We all slowly turned to look at the big house behind us and the kitchen windows that overlooked the garden. Had

Bobby Chang, famous chef, plotted murder in that very room last night?

Yasmine's dark eyes grew wide. "Why would he do that?"

"She *was* pretty cranky." Cho nodded, as if that explained it.

Fitz sniffed. "You must admit that hardly seems enough motive for murder."

"Yeah, and had Bobby even met Irene before this? If not, what motive could he possibly have?" I frowned as I cast back in my memory. Florence had introduced each of us yesterday afternoon and explained our roles—influencers, travel writer, food blogger, and then all of us from the tearoom. But she hadn't explained the reason for Irene's presence.

"You know, the rest of being here makes sense, but Irene stood out. Why was she here during the opening weekend?"

"Good point." Fitz's gaze grew far away—his deep in thought look.

Dom's low voice drew my attention. "Would the chef risk this place to kill?"

That did seem to go against Bobby's own interests.

Fitz gazed up at the gorgeous, imposing manor house. "A murder, even a natural death, threatens to mar his opening weekend."

Bobby would have to have a strong reason, more than mere annoyance, to kill Irene and jeopardize everything he'd built here at Bulbrook Manor.

Leo flipped a hand. "He does seem obsessed with this place."

It was true, and yet...

I glanced at Ellie, who stood off a ways, speaking with Olwen, Janisa, and Karine. "This place isn't the *only* thing Bobby's overly into." I raised my brows. "Did you guys notice him and Florence?"

I explained what I'd seen after we arrived yesterday

afternoon. "I think Irene caught Florence and Bobby having a little 'private time' in the stables. They all booked it out of there with red faces."

Cho gaped. "So maybe Bobby killed Irene to keep her from exposing his affair?"

I shrugged. "Maybe."

Fitz raised a brow. "He's hardly being discreet, though. This morning, in his room?"

I snapped my fingers. "That's right, I'd forgotten. Ellie and Bobby have separate rooms, which doesn't on its own mean much, but I think Bobby had someone in his bed this morning. Someone who wasn't Ellie."

Yas curled her lip. "Yikes."

Boom!

I jumped, and Janisa shrieked as a huge thunderclap split the air. Ellie sucked in a breath over her teeth.

"We'd best pack it in."

I'd been so absorbed in this talk over Irene's death, I hadn't noticed the uptick in the wind, the thick clouds blotting out the light overhead, or the drop in temperature. Another roll of thunder sounded nearby, and we hurried to store our smocks and gloves back in the garage beside the parked Land Rover.

I hung back a little to pull Gus aside in the garage. "Hey!" I waved him over.

My stylish bestie tossed aside his frock—how did he manage to look high fashion in a gardening apron?—and told Kurt he'd catch up to him, then sauntered over. "Yes, Minnie?"

My heart quickened with a mix of fear and annoyance. "Listen, if you're distracting Kurt to keep him away from the rest of us, I guess I appreciate it, but..."

He crossed his arms and glared down his straight nose at me.

I licked my lips and shot him an exasperated look. "But

come on—what the heck is going on between you two? Is that it? Are you actually like—friends?" I flashed my eyes at him and splayed my hands, hoping for some kind of reasonable explanation. "Because, ridiculous as it sounds, it kind of seems like you might actually be friends." I scoffed, waiting for him to join in.

Instead he glared down at me and tipped his head. "Is it ridiculous?"

I crossed my arms, mimicking his closed-off posture. "Umm, yeah it would be kinda crazy for a—" I checked around to make sure no one was within earshot. "A vampire to befriend a vampire hunter."

He shook his head and started back toward the manor house. "I thought you were taking a break from snooping this weekend, Minnie."

I followed him, half-jogging to keep up with his long strides. Anger flashed hot in my chest. "First of all, it's *sleuthing* that I'm taking a break from, and secondly, it's not snooping to be interested in my best friend's life."

The first sprinkles pattered my head and arms as we hurried across the lawn, rejoining the others. I shot Gus a "this conversation is to be continued" look, and he responded by rolling his eyes. Great.

I leapt up the steps with everyone else and dashed into the lounge. Ellie was the last inside. She closed the french doors behind her and locked them. Lightning flashed in the black storm clouds that blanketed the sky all the way to the horizon.

Our hostess turned and let out a heavy sigh. "Looks like none of us will be leaving the house for the rest of the weekend."

11

BOBBY

"I'm starving." I squeezed Fitz's arm.

He grinned and eyed my stomach. "I know."

I pressed a hand to my grumbling belly and shot him a playful grin. "Har har. Seriously, though, as hungry as I am, I'm a little nervous. Is it safe to eat? Prescott asked some questions about our meals yesterday, and after what Ellie said about those mushrooms..."

He sobered. "That's a fair point."

Fitz pulled our friends aside and together we formed a plan. While our friends distracted Ellie and Florence in the dining room, Dom, Fitz, and I snuck over toward the kitchen.

We slipped around the dividing wall, and I glanced back. Using the mirror on the wall across from the table I checked and made sure our exit hadn't been noticed.

We crept into the massive kitchen and quietly shut the door behind us. Bobby worked with his head down over the stove in a white chef's jacket. "Fifteen minutes," he called, without looking up.

Dom cleared his throat—somehow making it sound

intimidating—and Bobby whipped his surprised gaze around to look at us. "Oh, hey—sorry, but guests aren't supposed to be in here."

He dried his hands on the apron around his waist as something cheesy and onion-y sizzled in a big pan on the stove. My mouth watered, and I almost backed out of the plan. The food smelled so good, who cared if it was a little poisoned, right? I shook myself, willed my hangry brain to cooperate, and approached the huge island.

I placed my hands on the marble countertop and stood behind one of the dozen stools lined up around it. Bobby had mentioned cooking classes, and it seemed that the giant kitchen, with its three ovens and oversized range, must have been designed with teaching in mind. The double-wide stainless steel fridge gleamed, as did all the brand-new appliances and shining countertops. This place had to be heaven for a chef, especially with the floor-to-ceiling windows looking out over the lush garden.

"We just need a quick word, Bobby."

He frowned. "I'm in the middle of cooking."

I sucked on my lips. "Yeah, that's why we need to talk to you now."

The chef's brow furrowed in confusion, and Fitz licked his lips. "You see, we believe Irene Fernsby may have been poisoned by mushrooms."

Bobby continued to frown at him until Fitz gave him a significant look, and the chef's face drained of color. "Oh—oh! Bloody..." He covered his mouth with a scarred hand and blinked at us, his expression full of horror. "You don't think—you mean—the mushrooms from dinner?"

Dom folded his arms and stared the man down. He might be a murderer, but his terrified reaction seemed genuine. If he'd killed Irene, my gut told me it'd been accidental.

I softened my tone. "Ellie pointed out some death cap

mushrooms on the foraging hike—they really do look exactly like safely edible ones." I winced. "She said you gathered the mushrooms for yesterday's dinner and Irene had jaundice, which I guess is a symptom of death cap poisoning."

"Oh no no no no no. I'm going to be sick." Bobby dragged both hands through his thick black hair.

Fitz plucked up a stool and placed it in the kitchen, then guided Bobby to sit on it. Probably a good idea—I feared he might be about to faint.

His breath came in short pants as he gaped, stricken. "I'm an experienced chef, how could I have made that mistake?" He groaned. "I swear to you, I'm positive the mushrooms I gathered were safe."

Dom raised a brow, and Bobby whimpered.

"At least, I *thought* I was sure."

I couldn't help but feel sympathy for the poor man. He seemed genuinely distraught at the idea that he might've caused Irene's death.

"Wait—is anyone else sick?"

I shook my head and he blinked.

"Only Irene?" He frowned down at the stained apron in his lap. "But how could that be?"

I bit my lip. "Maybe she was already sick and more sensitive to them, or she got a higher concentration of poisonous mushrooms mixed in among the safe ones?"

He shook his head. "No... I gathered them all from the same spot. They would've all been the same kind."

Fitz leveled him an intense look. "To be clear, you did not intentionally poison that older lady?"

Bobby's cheeks reddened. "What? No! Why would you think that?"

I shifted on my feet. "This is awkward but... we've all noticed the er, friendly looks—"

"And touches," Dom interjected.

"—between you and Florence. I know Irene did too."

Bobby's face turned the color of a tomato.

"What's the hold up— oh." Florence stepped through the door behind us and froze. "Ah, this area is off-limits to guests. I'm afraid you all will need to—" She jerked her head toward the door to the dining room, but Bobby shook his head.

Fitz lifted his chin. "We needed to have a word with Mr. Chang about the safety of today's meal."

Florence frowned as we explained our concern about the mushrooms, and as we finished, she collapsed onto one of the stools herself. "Oh no."

Fitz shot her a sympathetic look. "I'm afraid it's a very real possibility that Irene was killed by Mr. Chang's cooking."

"We'd prefer not to be next," Dom growled. "In case he'd like to silence us, as well."

"We know about you two." I gestured between Florence and Bobby, and the blond manager turned bright red. She and Bobby matched.

Florence cringed. "You're not going to tell Ellie, are you?"

Dom, Fitz, and I looked at each other. I believed in telling the truth. At the same time, it didn't seem our place. I pressed my lips together and hedged our bets. "That depends on whether it's relevant to Irene's death." I shot a challenging look at Bobby.

The chef raised his palms, as if surrendering. "Listen, I didn't kill her... at least not on purpose, okay?"

Dom sniffed. "How reassuring."

"There's no way I would risk the opening weekend like that. This place is my whole life, okay?" Bobby pressed a hand to the breast of his white jacket. "I'd rather an affair come out than a client die of food poisoning, to be honest. I mean, that doesn't look great for a professional chef, right?

Who's going to want to come eat healthy, chef-prepared food if the chef is killing people, huh?"

He had a point.

He pleaded with us. "Look, I've put everything I own into this place, and then some—it's my passion project, my dream come true. All this—these renovations to fix this place up"—he gestured around the high-end kitchen—"it took way longer and cost *way* more than we'd planned, alright? It was hard." His throat bobbed. "Me and Ellie put every last cent and all our time and energy into this place and, well, it drove a wedge between us."

Florence sucked on her lips, clearly uncomfortable.

Bobby shrugged. "Ellie's not happy in this marriage, either. But this place, Bulbrook Grove? This is my last chance. It's my everything. Setting aside my own personal morals around murdering old ladies, I'm not gonna risk this place to keep an affair quiet."

Yeesh. A heavy weight settled in the pit of my stomach. Getting this place off the ground sounded like a Herculean effort, and I could understand how that might be hard on a marriage. If Bobby was as invested in this place as he claimed, I couldn't see him risking it to kill Irene. Not on purpose, at least.

I guess he still might've accidentally served us poisoned mushrooms, but like he'd said—they'd all been harvested from the same spot. If Bobby had accidentally cooked with poisonous mushrooms, it stood to reason that we'd all have fallen ill.

"I'm going to head back out. Everyone's starving." Florence slid off the stool and smoothed her blazer.

Bobby moved back to the stove. "Food will be up soon—ten minutes."

We moved to follow Florence, but I had another thought. "Bobby—if this place tanked, couldn't you go work at another posh restaurant? You're a famous chef, after all, right?"

He stirred the delicious-smelling concoction on the stove, his face red. "This isn't the first time."

I gawked. "That you've killed somebody?"

He rolled his eyes at me. "That I've... strayed. I cheated on Ellie a couple years ago with a server in the restaurant I worked at. My wife found out, and we decided to move to the country for a fresh start."

We hovered near the door to the dining room as Bobby addressed us across the kitchen island. "My reputation in the industry took a hit. Not that an affair is uncommon but... Ellie made a scene, and the messiness of it all—no one wants to touch me with a ten-foot pole. *This* was supposed to be my and Ellie's fresh start. I need to make this work or I'll lose it all." He wrung his hands. "Look, we'll figure out what happened to Irene, but I promise you, her death was the last thing I wanted, not only for me, but for her sake, too. Poor lady. Her husband just died of lung cancer, and now she's dead? Tragic."

I narrowed my eyes. "Seriously?"

He nodded. "Yeah, she was my mom's neighbor. Irene was always getting on my mom's case for minor HOA infractions—a total nightmare. Mom hated her, until she learned Irene's story, and then she pitied her, you know. They became, not exactly friends, but sympathetic." He grabbed the handle of the pan and tossed the sizzling contents.

"Well, anyway, we had a last-minute cancellation for the opening, and my mom begged me to offer the spot to Irene. She thought the poor lady could use a peaceful weekend." He sighed and shook his head at the stove, turning off a knob, grabbing a spatula and opening the oven door in such fluid, practiced movements, that I had no doubt of his vast experience as a chef. "Poor lady ended up dying here."

Again, my witchy intuition told me Bobby was in

earnest. I sighed. I guess that explained Irene's presence this weekend and why she didn't seem to fit in with the rest of us. I pointed at the chef. "Alright, just... no more mushrooms."

The chef scoffed. "Oh gawd, no."

12

VAMPIRE VITAMINS

After a tense meal, we were given about an hour of free time before afternoon water aerobics class. While I was eager to check out the indoor pool—the brochure photos looked beautiful—I was already exhausted from the restless night and foraging hike this morning.

Once back in our room, I threw myself on the bed, wrinkling the comforter Fitz had so neatly made, and heaved a weary sigh. "You know, I thought this was going to be a relaxing weekend. Now Gus and I are fighting, Kurt's here, and that poor woman's been killed." As if to punctuate my thoughts, a huge thunderclap boomed outside. I whimpered with anxiety, thinking of my little familiar. "I hope Tilda's okay. She hates storms."

Fitz lowered himself onto the edge of the bed and took my hand. "I'm sure Mim is taking great care to keep her comfortable."

I nodded, staring up at the high, molded ceiling. "You're right. She's probably whipped her up some magically calming cat treats, or something."

Fitz smiled and squeezed my hand. "Do you want to call and check on her?"

I rolled onto my side to face him and propped my head in my hand. "I do, but later. I've got Irene's death on my mind."

Fitz fought a smile. "You don't say? Color me shocked."

I shot him a flat look, and he chuckled, then stroked my cheek with his thumb. "I'm teasing. I appreciate your sharp, curious mind... even if it and your many misadventures do cause me to feel deeply concerned at times."

I nodded. I didn't blame him. I'd had enough run-ins with killers and creeps that I worried for myself sometimes, too. I grinned up at his handsome face. "At least this time, we're together." I poked his arm. "So you can help me talk this out."

He smiled and nodded for me to continue.

I pushed myself up to sitting. Despite it being only early afternoon, the dark clouds made the day feel many hours later than it was. I drew on my magic, snapped my fingers, and all the candles in the room burst into flame, giving us more light.

Fitz's eyes widened. "Nicely done."

My cheeks warmed. "Why, thank you." Big raindrops pattered the window and formed ripples on the surface of the swollen river across the lawn.

I was about to launch into my thoughts on Irene's odd death when a knock sounded at the door. Fitz swept over and opened it to a little grouping of our buddies.

"Can we come in?" Cho led the way into the room, followed by Leo, Dom, and a downcast Calvin. No Gus, though. I supposed he was off somewhere hanging out with his *new* friend and risking his own life in the process. I set my jaw and tried to put it out of mind. "Where are Yasmine and Al?"

Cho shrugged and slumped into the desk chair. "Probably in their room. We didn't see them."

Dom leaned against the wall by the door, crossing his massive arms and looking stoic as always, while the downcast Calvin slid down the wall and crossed his legs on the thick rug. Fitz and Leo perched on the bed beside me.

"Well, you guys have good timing—I was about to go over my theories with Fitz."

"Oh, phew." Cho made a show of wiping his brow. "Thank goodness we didn't miss that."

I glared at him. "Careful, or I'll throw a pillow at you."

He chuckled, while Leo wrung his hands and nodded to himself. "Something's up—I can feel it."

I pointed at my friend. "Yep. Me, too." I lifted a palm. "If we believe Bobby, then he might've cooked with poisonous mushrooms and killed Irene on accident—but it seems like some others of us would've gotten at least a little sick."

Dom nodded.

Cho made a face. "Come on, guys. I mean it's sad, sure, but couldn't she have died of old age? Are we sure she even got poisoned?"

Fitz rolled his shirtsleeves. "Perhaps, but the jaundice is odd. She might've experienced sudden organ failure, but the timing is suspicious."

I nodded. "And I saw her the night before clutching her stomach, remember?" I checked my phone but hadn't missed a call or text from Prescott. "Prescott's going to keep me and Kurt in the loop, so we should know pretty soon if he suspects foul play."

"Hypothetically, if Irene *was* targeted, why would anyone want to kill her?" Leo shrugged.

"And how?" Fitz gave me a significant look. "Aside from Bobby Chang, no one had met her before this weekend, giving very few clues as to a motive. Plus, the chef was the only person in the kitchen."

Leo pointed at him. "Except for Ellie—she was serving."

"Irene was cranky, but we've all dealt with worse customers at the tearoom and managed not to kill them." Cho scrunched up his face. "Why would Bobby have done that?"

"I believe Irene deserves some leeway for her dudgeon—Bobby informed us that her husband had recently passed away of cancer." Fitz pressed his lips together.

Cho shot my boyfriend an incredulous look. "Her *what*?"

Fitz's vampirically pale face blushed slightly pink with embarrassment. "Er, it means her bad mood."

"Wait—that's right!" Something in my mind slid into place, and I bounced in place. "Irene was asking all those pointed questions about Janisa's cancer treatment at dinner last night, remember?"

Dom nodded, and Leo made a thoughtful noise. "Oh right, she did."

"*And* I overheard raised voices in Janisa and Karine's room on the way to supper last night. Irene was chewing them out, saying something about Janisa needing to come clean about being a fraud—that she was going to hurt a lot of innocent people if she didn't."

Cho, who sat backward in the desk chair, drummed his fingers on it. "Yeah, they were pretty peeved about it last night at the—" He grew sheepish. "At the after-hours party. They were talking about what a crazy old lady she is... er, was."

Leo—obviously still peeved about not getting an invite—scowled at him, and Cho pretended not to notice.

Dom parted his pouty, full lips. "Think Janisa is faking?"

I raised my brows at him, then Fitz. "I know it sounds awful but... maybe?"

"No way." Cho scoffed. "Janisa's super nice, you guys. You just don't know her like I do."

"And whose fault is that?" Leo flashed his eyes. "Maybe if you'd told me about this secret party of yours..."

Cho rolled his eyes. "Then it wouldn't be a secret, would it?"

I crossed my arms. "Come on, Cho, spill it. What happened last night?"

Dom glowered at him, and Cho gulped. "Fine. Serena invited a select few VIPs to her room. It was me, her, Janisa, and Karine." Cho pulled his lips to the side. "We hung out and talked, and Janisa told us more about her story and all her followers and her new wellness tea coming out. And Serena was like, oh cool, I have a vitamin pack, and they were all like we should do a collaboration, and then Serena gave us some free samples."

Leo raised a questioning brow. "Serena makes her own vitamin packs?"

Cho shrugged. "Well, she said she lives in some commune or something, and they make it there. You add the powder to water—it's orange flavored—and I swear I felt like fifty times more alert, stronger—I could even hear better."

I gaped at him, flabbergasted, as Dom dropped his head and pinched the bridge of his nose. Leo shook his head. "You dummy, I told you she was a vampire."

"So?"

I shot him a disbelieving look. "So, you went to a vampire's room, late at night, and drank some of her mysterious powder."

Cho scoffed. "Fitz is a vampire."

My boyfriend blew out a heavy breath, and I flashed my eyes at my friend. "Yeah, but you know Fitz. You have no idea if Serena's a friendly vamp or an 'I'll eat your throat' vamp!"

He winced, finally looking a bit chastened. "I guess you guys have a point. I dunno—I figured she's a yoga teacher and all Zen and stuff. She couldn't be violent... right?"

Fitz extended his hand. "May I see the vitamin packet?"

Cho half stood and rummaged around in his jeans pockets, then handed over an orange square, a couple of inches long on each side. It had professional packaging, and I wouldn't have questioned it had I spotted it on a shelf at the grocery store.

Fitz looked it over. "The description is quite vague."

Leo made grabby hands for it, and Fitz passed it over to the lion shifter. The stocky guy ripped the top off, licked his finger, then dabbed some powder on his fingertip and tasted it. "Ugh." He made a face and raked his tongue across the roof of his mouth. "That does not taste right."

"Did you miss the part about adding water?"

I passed the vitamin powder back to Fitz, who delicately sniffed at the packet, then paled—which was something for the vampire. His nostrils flared. "There's dried vamp blood in here."

My jaw dropped. So Kurt was right about Serena using the wellness center to recruit new vampires!

"I knew it was off!" Leo jabbed a finger at Cho. He'd clearly detected that extra ingredient with his supernaturally sharp sense of taste.

Fitz shot Cho a grim look. "That's why you feel brilliant. Vampire blood, even in powdered form, can dramatically heal a human and even enhance one's senses, strength, and stamina."

Cho winced, his voice small. "That doesn't sound *so* bad."

Fitz's throat bobbed, a muscle in his jaw jumping with barely restrained anger. "It's temporary and often leaves the consumer desperately craving more once the effects subside." He turned to me, eyes blazing. "Serena is getting humans addicted to vampire blood."

"Ew. Why?" Cho grimaced. "Actually, now that you mention it, she *did* try to convince us to join her commune for further 'treatments.'"

Leo threw his hands in the air like he couldn't believe Cho's gullibility.

Fitz shook his head. "This is reminiscent of a scam Darius liked to perform during my time living with him."

Fitz's vampire sire, Darius—who also happened to be head of Bath's local vampire council—ruled over a nest of vampires—people he turned with or without their consent, and then demanded servitude from. Fitz had been trapped in that cycle for decades before he'd been able to barely buy his freedom. Even now, he was still building his life back, and I could see now that his anger didn't lie with Cho, or even necessarily Serena, but with whoever was at the helm of this scam.

"You think it could be Darius behind all this?"

Fitz nodded slowly, his intense gaze faraway. "I think it's quite likely, yes."

"Could this have something to do with Irene's death?"

Fitz furrowed his brow as he considered the question. "While I believe Darius is capable of just about any level of villainy, in this case, I'm not sure I see how he or his vitamin powder could be involved."

I had to agree. Irene hadn't attended yoga, supper, or the party last night. It seemed unlikely she'd even crossed paths with Serena. Besides, if anything, the healing powers of the dried vampire blood would probably have only helped her.

I folded the packet closed and shoved it in the pocket of my jeans. Thunder rumbled, and lightning flashed across the dark sky outside the huge window. I sighed. "We have a lot of questions, and not too many answers—yet." I patted my thighs. "But, it sounds like Irene thought Janisa was faking her cancer and confronted her about it."

Leo nodded. "Definitely."

"Hmm." I pulled my phone up and searched until I found Janisa's social media. She had a massive following—this girl was a legit influencer—with thousands of perfectly posed and lighted pictures. She'd even shared some from our weekend already. I poked around her account.

"Janisa has some major brand deals, and her beating cancer seems to be a big part of her overall brand." I tipped my head, thoughtful. "She has a lot of money tied into that. It would ruin her life and career if Irene exposed her as a phony."

Fitz grinned at me. "Sounds like you have a suspect."

Right. But how to go about questioning her?

Leo checked his smart watch. "Hate to say it, guys, but we've got water aerobics soon."

Dom pushed off the wall and jerked his head toward the door. "Let's go." He reached down and grabbed Calvin, who'd been sulking the whole time, by the back of his jacket and hauled him to his feet.

Actually, this might give me the perfect opportunity to get more information out of Janisa.

13

LOCKER ROOM TALK

"Just the witch I wanted to see." I linked my arm through Yasmine's on our way to the pool and filled her in on our suspicions about Janisa faking her cancer. I also showed her the vitamin packet Serena had given Cho.

Yas tossed her beach towel over her shoulder and gave me a wry grin. "Maybe I should've gone to that party, after all." We moved slowly down the hall, Yasmine now leaning heavily on me. "Maybe a little supernatural pick me up would do me some good."

I pressed my lips together, sympathetic. I knew she wasn't serious about the vampire blood, but I wished there was some other way I could help my friend. "Are you feeling that hike and the gardening today? That was a lot, huh?"

She nodded and rolled her eyes. "It's my own fault—I pushed myself too hard, but I was having fun."

I shot her a questioning look as we stepped into the women's locker room. "Are you going to be okay doing water aerobics?"

She snorted. "I'd pass out. No, my plan is to lounge in the jacuzzi." She gave a serene smile, and I grinned.

"That's not a bad idea."

"Wow." Yas's eyes widened in surprise as we rounded the corner and stepped into the beautifully lit, Zen room. Wooden lockers lined the walls, plush robes hung from hooks on the tiled walls, and round ring light mirrors hung over the marble vanity. Of course, Janisa sat in a fluffy white robe with one shoulder exposed, perched on a stool at the vanity. She posed as Karine snapped pics for her. We set our bags down on the nearest bench, and Karine waved. "Hey, girls!"

We waved back, and as I slipped out of my shoes, I gasped. "Even the marble floors are heated."

Yas let out a wistful sigh. "Can we move in here?"

I changed into my cute new one piece, slid into one of the soft complimentary robes and rubber slides, and then opened a locker to stash my stuff inside. To my surprise, someone else's belongings already occupied the space. My first instinct was to close it and look for an open locker, but I hesitated and glanced over my shoulder. With the girls distracted by taking pics, I nudged Yas.

"I think this is Janisa's bag," I whispered. I was pretty sure I'd seen her carrying it at one point yesterday.

Yas raised a confused brow.

I didn't feel great about this, but my curiosity got the best of me. "Keep an eye out."

She planted her hands on her hips and looked exasperated but turned her back to me as I'd asked. I tugged the twill bucket bag open. Various patches and buttons covered the outside, and the inside was a mess. I dug through pill cases, pens, bags of makeup and rifled past her wallet. I knew it wasn't cool to snoop like this, but what if Janisa had something to do with Irene's death? We didn't know for sure that Irene had been killed, yet, but my witchy intuition told me something suspicious was up.

My fingers wrapped around a plastic baggy and I pulled

it out for a quick look. I moved the little dried brown contents around, not quite sure what I was looking at, until it clicked.

I patted Yas's shoulder and held up the baggie. "Look," I hissed. "Mushrooms!"

"Hey!"

I jerked my head up to find Janisa and Karine gawking at me.

"What are you doing? That's mine." The girls leapt to their feet and marched up to us.

The blond reached out to snatch the baggie from me, but I jumped back, holding it out of reach. She gaped at me, then Karine. "Can you believe her? This is theft; I'm calling the police."

I snorted. "If I don't call them on *you* first."

Janisa and Karine both looked put out. "Excuse me?"

Yas sucked on her lips like she hoped I knew what I was doing. I hoped so, too.

I shook the dried mushrooms. "Did you put these in Irene's food last night?"

The whites showed around Janisa's blue eyes. "Are you crazy?"

Karine lifted her phone and snapped a picture of me, the flash temporarily causing spots to float across my vision. "I'm filming now. This is evidence that you are being crazy."

I shifted on my feet, afraid I'd made a mistake. This was not the "gotcha" moment I'd expected.

Yas cleared her throat and quietly added, "Janisa, you were sitting next to Irene. It would've been possible to slip some of those into her dish."

"They were next to each other?" I cast back in my memory. I knew Irene sat close to the fire at dinner, but was that beside Janisa?

Yas nodded, and I held the baggie up higher. I'd take her word for it. I turned back to Janisa. "Is that what you did?

Found some poisonous mushrooms, snuck them onto Irene's plate, and killed her?"

Janisa folded her arms over her robe and shot me a withering look. "Those are magic mushrooms, you dork. You know, hallucinogens?"

I took a closer look at the dried brown bits in the bag.

Karine nodded, and the curls piled on top of her head bounced. "They can be used for really deep spiritual work."

The blond influencer smirked. "Or a good time. I brought them in case anyone wanted to take them with me. No way would I waste them on that old lady." She sobered. "I mean, rest in peace, or whatever."

Yas's cheeks turned bright pink, and she shot me a horrified look. I winced. "So... these aren't poisonous?"

The girls shot me disparaging looks, like they'd never seen anyone so pathetic. "No."

I sucked in a breath and stared Janisa down, making one last-ditch attempt to intimidate her. "How are we supposed to believe you?"

She made an annoyed growl in the back of her throat, snatched the baggie from me, and then reached in and popped a small chunk into her mouth. She chewed the mushroom piece, then opened her mouth wide to show us that she'd swallowed it. "See?"

My face flushed hot, and I wished I could melt into the floor out of embarrassment. I'd have to ask Mim if there was a spell for that. "Oh."

Karine clicked her tongue. "Why did you think Janisa killed that old lady?"

"Yeah?" Janisa crossed her arms and shot me a challenging look.

I was in this far already, might as well push on. "I overheard the argument you two had with Irene last night. She called you a fraud."

Janisa looked bored, but Karine shook her head. "Okay,

yeah, that happened. But it wouldn't be hard for Janisa to prove her innocence and that she really did see all those doctors for her cancer. That lady was kinda crazy."

Janisa nodded, though she kept her eyes down on her feet. "Mm-hmm." My witchy senses tingled. The more I worked on my magic, the stronger my intuition seemed to grow. My gut told me Janisa was lying.

I scoffed. "Irene was right, wasn't she? You never had cancer."

Yasmine flashed her eyes at me, and I didn't blame her. That was a big accusation—and one I'd deeply regret if I was wrong. I'd been totally off base with the mushroom thing, so I hoped Yas would still be my friend after this played out.

Janisa glared at me. "I don't have to answer you. You don't have any proof of that, and neither did that old lady." Her voice had an aggressive, biting edge I hadn't heard from the airy influencer before.

Karine seemed surprised, too, as she gawked at her boss friend.

I stepped closer, feeling less than formidable in my swimsuit and fluffy robe, but I threw my shoulders back and glared at her. "Irene sniffed you out. Her husband actually had lung cancer and died of it. She asked you about all the specialist doctors he saw, but it was obvious you were clueless about them. She realized it then and called you out as a fraud."

Doubt crept into Karine's expression.

I pointed at Janisa. "You killed Irene to keep her from exposing you."

Janisa's voice dripped with contempt. "Exposing me?" She barked out a humorless laugh. "How exactly, would she have done that? She was like a million years old—she didn't have social media! I bet she didn't even know how to work a smartphone." She rolled her eyes. "So who would she tell exactly?" She caught Karine's shocked expression and turned bright red. "I—I mean—even if she was right." She blinked rapidly, her words faltering. "Which, like, she wasn't."

Wow. I didn't even need my magical truth serum or witchy intuition to know she was lying—she was bad at it. How had Janisa gotten away with it for so long? Probably no one had ever challenged her on the details before.

Karine pressed a hand to her chest. "I'm actually sick—I have a thyroid condition. I believed you!"

Janisa looked away and scratched the side of her mouth. "As you should."

Karine shook her head. "I've been working for you, for *free*, for months, and you made it all up, didn't you?" She smacked her own forehead. "I'm such a dope. It all makes sense now. Whenever you talked about your cancer you were always messing up your timeline, you had no records, and you never let me meet any of your family or anyone who knew you growing up. I chalked it up to you being quirky and a little air-headed."

"Hey now!" the influencer jutted her chin out.

"What the heck, Janisa?" Karine threw her hands up. "I believed your protocol and your teas would cure me!"

Janisa twirled the end of her ponytail. "Um... they like, totally will."

"No, they won't!" Karine stomped her rubber-sandaled foot. "All they do is make me poop!"

I caught Yasmine's eye and thumbed toward the pool. "On that note, we should probably get to water aerobics."

Yasmine slammed her locker shut, and we booked it out of the locker room, leaving Janisa and Karine, still loudly bickering, behind.

14

WATER AEROBICS

I bounced around in the pool, wincing as Cho splashed some water in my eye. I raised my arms overhead, following Serena's lead as she stood on the deck above us. While I was not in the mood for more exercise—the hike this morning had been plenty—I had to admit the indoor pool had a neat ambience.

The slatted wooden ceiling curved and peaked high overhead, reminding me of the hull of an upturned ship. Soft, submerged lights gave the water a mystical blue glow. While two of the room's walls consisted of floor-to-ceiling windows, the dark storm clouds let in only a dim, gloomy light, and though the windows probably normally framed a stunning view of the valley, heavy rain now lashed against the glass, completely obscuring the outside. Except for the occasional flash of lightning that streaked across the sky, of course.

"And three—two—one." Serena lowered her arms and bounced in place. "Let your arms relax but stay on your toes and keep moving."

Janisa curled her lip and shot a wary glance at the

windows where another bolt of lightning flashed. "Aren't we not supposed to be swimming during a thunderstorm?"

She and Karine had emerged, sulking, from the locker room just as class started and had moved to opposite ends of the long pool from each other.

Karine rolled her eyes and called out, "That's only if you're outside, *obviously*."

They glared across the twenty-five-meter pool at each other, then seemed to find a mutual distraction in Dom's bare, tattooed chest. He stood in the middle, oblivious to all the attention he was getting from the influencers, as well as Serena and even Olwen, who I was pretty sure had said she was married. I turned and caught Yasmine's eye. She and Al lounged in the steamy, bubbly jacuzzi, and she seemed to read my thoughts because she chuckled when our eyes met.

As Serena led us through our next exercises, I swam closer to Fitz and clued him in on what happened with Janisa in the locker room. I whispered, though with Serena's voice echoing around the big space, the splashes, and the low hum from the jacuzzi, I doubted anyone but those closest to me could overhear.

"I don't think Janisa did anything to Irene."

"Ha!" Cho smirked, his dark, wet hair slicked back from his face. "I told you she was nice, if you gave her a chance."

I shot him a withering look. "She all but admitted to faking cancer."

Cho's expression fell, and Leo shook his head as he splashed around in front of me. "That's cold."

Cho sighed. "Why is it always the hot ones?"

Was it, though?

More lightning flashed behind the solid sheet of rain pouring down the windows as gentle steam coiled up from the heated pool water. I was torn between finding the vibe cozy or creepy.

"Remember, try to kick hard enough to keep your shoulders above water." Serena directed her correction at Nathan, whose mind looked a million miles away. He'd been standing there, a crease worrying his brow, but Serena's voice seemed to snap him out of it. He shook it off and resumed treading water, though he still wore a preoccupied expression.

The travel writer had been jovial and talkative the day before, but now Serena kept having to remind him to be present. He seemed distracted. Maybe he was tired, like I was, or maybe Irene's death had hit him hard. It'd definitely been a big shock.

Cho panted as he kicked harder. "Was Jane Austen actually—into—water aerobics?"

This got a chuckle out of our lithe instructor. "Keep it up!" she called, her voice echoing around the open space.

"Actually," I managed to gasp out as I swished my arms through the water. "Sea bathing was big—during Austen's time."

Fitz nodded. "It was essentially bobbing around in the ocean."

I blinked, shocked for a moment that I'd forgotten my boyfriend actually lived through these times. Maybe it should've felt weird or off-putting, but I found it fascinating. It was always amazing to get his firsthand experiences of a time period I so admired.

Cho huffed, and I grinned at him, fighting to keep my chin out of the water. "The water would've been freezing—though."

Serena clearly overheard. "I could turn off the heater, Cho, if you're concerned about historical accuracy?"

His eyes widened, and he quickly shook his head, causing Serena to grin. I exchanged a surprised look with Fitz. Maybe Cho had a chance with her after all.

I glanced back over my wet shoulder and immediately wished I hadn't. Kurt playfully splashed Gus, who somehow looked even more ethereal and polished in his tight black swim pants, with his white-blond hair slicked back. My resentment for the hunter's intrusion on our weekend faded a bit as I noted the many scars snaking across his chest and arms.

I turned back around and pouted. I had to admit those two seemed to have fun together. In a perfect world, they could be friends and enjoy each other's company. But this was the real world, and how was I the only one who could see that a vampire and a hunter getting close would inevitably lead to disaster? Like, someone gets a stake in their chest or fangs in their neck, level disaster?

Fitz must've picked up on my mood, because he shot me a tight-lipped smile. Even seeing him in his buttoned-up striped bathing romper couldn't lighten my mood, now that I was back to brooding over Gus and Kurt.

I gave him a small smile back. I had to admit that while in the abstract I would've thought his old-fashioned suit hilarious, on Fitz's broad-shoulders and trim frame, it kind of did something for me. It didn't hurt that for something that covered from shoulders to knees it was surprisingly revealing—wet cotton did not leave much to the imagination.

Oh boy—now I was nervous again as I thought about the two of us sharing a room. Between Irene's death—probably murder—Kurt getting way too close to my friends, and my nerves around taking things to the next level with Fitz, this was not shaping up to be the restful weekend I'd hoped for.

∽

AFTER CLASS, I dried off, wrapped up in my robe and put on my rubber slides, then rejoined Yasmine, Olwen, Janisa, and Karine in the locker room. I changed back into my jeans and sweater. I'd just wound my long hair into a ballerina bun on top of my head, with a few damp tendrils stuck to my neck, when a thunderous *BOOM* made my stomach drop.

Janisa screamed, and the lights flickered out. I stood there for a moment in absolute darkness, my heart pounding, before I remembered my phone in my pocket. I tapped the flashlight feature and shone it around. The other gals did the same, illuminating the locker room in harsh, blue light.

"Everyone alright?" Olwen asked, her towel wrapped around her head.

As the most dressed, I volunteered to find Serena or one of the staff. "I'll check for her by the pool and see if she has an update on the situation." I nodded at Yasmine. "Be right back."

I slung my enormous leather bag over my shoulder, with my wet swimsuit bundled in a plastic grocery bag inside, and threaded through the dark locker room back to the pool. With the wall of windows, the light here was a bit brighter, though still dim. I blinked and scanned the edge of the pool. "Hello?"

The light from my phone fell over two figures entwined in the jacuzzi. "Sorry." My cheeks flushed hot with embarrassment, and I turned away, but then my mind registered what I'd seen, and I spun back. "Holy moly!"

Gus's wide eyes met mine, before he slumped lower under the water and covered his face with both hands. Beside him, Kurt held still for a beat before the pool lights flickered back on, along with the canned lights in the high, peaked ceiling.

I gaped at my vampire friend, shell-shocked—at an absolute loss for words. I'd thought it was bad enough that he was interested in Kurt as a *friend*. How had I not seen that it was more than that? I guessed it was because Kurt had talked about previous girlfriends and how he'd never met one who understood the vampire hunter lifestyle. I'd assumed he was only interested in women. But even if I'd known... the two of them together? This was insane.

Kurt clapped his hands together, his tone overly chipper. "Lights are back on."

I shook my head, gobsmacked. My arms had gone limp, and my bag slid off my shoulder, spilling its contents across the decking as it landed.

Perfect.

I crouched down to pick everything up, and Kurt sprung out of the jacuzzi and came close to help. As he picked up a pack of tissues and a lip gloss, he lowered his voice. "Apologies, Minnie."

I glanced up at him, unsure where he was going with this. "For what?"

His throat bobbed as his long hair dripped onto the decking. "I think I broke hunter code. I should've made sure you weren't into Gus before I went for it." He winced. "Sorry."

I raised a brow, surprised at his conciliatory attitude. Kurt was normally full of bravado and confidence—this was a side of him I hadn't seen before. Behind him, Gus had sunk underwater.

"I'm not interested in him like that, Gus is my friend —*just* a friend. Also, I'm clearly with Fitz." I narrowed my eyes. "But... I didn't think *you'd* be interested in him."

Kurt tipped his head to one side. "I've never been interested in someone like him before."

For a brief moment ice flooded my stomach—did he mean a vampire? Did he know?

He leaned closer and whispered, "I've only dated women until now, but there's something about Gustaf." A fond smile played at the corner of his lips.

I hoped he still felt that way when he realized he was canoodling with one of the creatures his family had hunted for generations. I let out a heavy sigh and forced myself to say, "Well, I hope it works out." I mean, I *did* hope that, I simply had zero expectations that it actually would.

Kurt smirked. "Thanks." His gaze grew intense as he snatched up the orange vitamin packet Cho had handed over. He examined it then held it up, eyes blazing. "What's this?"

Before I had a chance to reply, he lurched to his feet. "A word, Minnie?"

I cast one last glance back at Gus who was still hiding underwater, then followed Kurt out into the hallway. It was colder out here and lacked the familiar smell of pool chemicals. I wrapped my arms around me. "What?"

Boom! Another clap of thunder left me quaking and the lights once again flickered and died. *Great.*

"I hope they replaced the electric when they renovated this place," I grumbled, blinking as my eyes adjusted to the dim light let in by the windows further down the hall.

With his face framed by dripping wet hair, Kurt shook the packet at me. "Where did you get this?"

"Uh—"

"You're holding out on me, Minnie. I've seen these before—during another case I worked at a yoga retreat near here last year."

Shoot! I didn't want to incriminate Cho by revealing he'd given it to me, or have Kurt start investigating my friends. "Um... I found it. On the ground."

He crossed his scarred arms and shot me a contemptuous look. "You're a terrible liar."

I grimaced. "I know."

He rolled his eyes and softened his tone. "Do you know what this is?" He searched my face, concerned. "Did you take any?"

"No." I sighed. "And I'm not sure, but I think it might

have dried vampire blood in it—what do you know about it?"

He nodded. "My theory is there's this vampire cult in Bath." He shook the packet. "I think they're handing these out."

My stomach clenched. I did *not* need Kurt having another reason to sniff out vampires in Bath.

He bit his lip. "It's some vitamin powder baloney, but you're right, there's dried vampire blood in here." He licked a finger and dipped it in the powder, then tasted it. "Yep. I'd need to run lab tests to be sure, but it smacks of vamp blood."

I raised a brow, incredulous. "Seriously, you can taste it?"

He clapped me on the shoulder and winked. "You'll get there someday, kid."

I'd rather not.

I blinked. "Wait—you said a cult?"

He inched closer and lowered his voice. "Like I told you before, this group targets wellness retreats for impressionable people open to 'alternative thinking.'" He sniffed. "These people tend to believe in the occult and a host of wacky conspiracy theories."

I mean... witches, vampires, ghosts, and shifters were real, so they weren't totally wrong there. But that did explain why they might target these groups versus people in hospitals.

"Plus, they're people who are usually looking for ways to improve their health— aka, they're already ill. The powder obviously makes them feel great, superhuman even for a bit, but with diminishing returns. They literally get them addicted until they're desperate to feel better again—and volunteer to be turned."

I pressed a hand to my stomach, disturbed. I'd already heard most of this, of course, but I hadn't considered the end it might lead to.

Kurt talked with his hands. "Of course by then, they're brought fully into the vampire cult—and roped into the ranks."

This made me think of the way Fitz had been manipulated into serving Darius. Could he be the one behind these vitamin packets? "That's terrible."

Kurt nodded, holding my gaze. "So, want to tell me again who gave this to you?" My first thought was to continue to play dumb about where I'd gotten the vitamin packet from. But then I hesitated. Kurt was on the scent now, which put Gus, Fitz, and all of my supernatural friends in even more danger. If I told him about Serena giving out the packets, he'd no doubt discover she was the vampire. While it would draw the heat off my friends, it would obviously put her in danger.

Would that be such a bad thing? My stomach twisted. She wasn't a good vampire, right, if she was trying to lure unsuspecting souls into a vampire cult? It'd be the easiest thing, to tell Kurt about her and let him handle it. My mouth went dry. I knew his method of handling it would mean killing Serena.

That was a dark thought. And what if she was a victim herself, like Fitz had been a victim of Darius, forced to do his bidding? I didn't know the full story and couldn't, in good conscience, expose her to Kurt. Even if it would make my life safer and easier.

I licked my lips and stuck with my earlier story. "I told you—I found it on the ground."

Kurt leveled me with a searching look for a long moment before he snatched the vitamin packet from me. "I'll hold on to this. If you discover anything else..."

I nodded as he headed back into the pool room. "You'll be the first to know."

15

LIGHTS OUT

Deep breaths, Minnie, deep breaths. If only I had a paper bag to hyperventilate into. Gathering myself, I smoothed my damp hair back and followed Kurt back into the pool area. I stepped through the door and ran right into a solid, cold wall of vampire.

I stumbled back as Gus reached out to steady me. As soon as I found my footing, I glared at him, and his concerned expression turned flat.

"Where's your boyfriend?" Ripple patterned reflections played off the empty pool area's ceiling.

Gus waited a beat, in which I thought he might deny it, but then he sighed. "Kurt headed to the locker room." He arched a brow. "And to be clear, he's not my boyfriend."

Lightning flashed outside the window, and the stark light briefly lit up the pool. *Boom!* The deafening thunderclap landed a moment later, and I jumped.

I glanced back, double-checking we were alone, then stepped closer to my bestie. "Look, I know you don't want to hear it, but what you're doing is certifiably crazy." I jabbed a finger at the now empty jacuzzi. "It was bad enough when I thought you two were becoming friends, but *that*? What the heck was that, Gus? Are you dating him now? Have you forgotten that he's a vampire hunter and would—nay, *will* try to kill you as soon as he inevitably finds out what you are? Do you have a death wish or something?"

My pale friend planted a hand on his hip, his open fluffy robe revealing his bare chest and swim tights. "Are you done?"

My heart pounded in my chest, and my face and chest burned hot, but I crossed my arms and shrugged.

"Has it ever occurred to you that I did not survive as long as I have by being a fool?"

I lifted my chin. Gus wouldn't even tell me how old he was, but I suspected he'd lived a long time as a vampire. Longer than Fitz, for sure, and Fitz had been turned in the early 1800s. "You have to admit, getting mixed up with an actual vampire *hunter* isn't the smartest thing for a vampire," I hissed.

He stalked closer, his eyes narrowed and nostrils flared. "Did I ask for your advice?"

He kept his voice low and steady, but it hit like a punch to the gut. Gus was really upset with me. We'd never fought this badly before, and my stomach tensed with stress. I hated this, I hated offending him, but did he not see what a horrible idea this was?

I huffed and threw my hands up. "No, you didn't *ask* for my advice, but you're my best friend, Gus. I'm trying to look out for you."

He sniffed. "Thank you, *very much*, but I can look out for myself."

"There you guys are."

I whirled toward the voice. Bobby stood at the pool's entrance, with Ellie and Florence flanking him. They each carried multiple electric camping lanterns in their hands.

Gus and I exchanged hard looks, and without a word, declared a truce for now. My friend swept over to our hosts as other guests emerged from the locker rooms. I hurried over to Fitz, back in his typical breeches and waistcoat, and threw my arms around him. He hugged me back and whispered against the top of my head, "Has something happened?"

I nodded. "I'll explain later." I needed the comfort of my boyfriend's arms around me. I hated arguing with Gus like this, but I just couldn't understand why he refused to listen to reason. Maybe it wasn't *technically* my business to voice my opinion on his relationship—or whatever it was with Kurt—but friends were supposed to tell you when you were doing something self-destructive, right?

Besides, if Kurt found out what Gus was, he'd naturally question whether I was aware, and that would blow my whole vampire hunter cover story, putting me, Fitz, and possibly the rest of my supernatural friends at risk.

We joined the little group gathered around Bobby, Ellie, and Florence as they passed out the golden-flamed oil lanterns. I shot little looks at Gus, but he steadfastly refused to meet my gaze. I huffed and did my best to put our feud out of my mind.

"It looks like we're out of power," Florence explained. "So you'll need these lanterns for the rest of the evening."

"We've already tried the breakers." Ellie sighed. "And we have a backup generator, but it's only got enough strength to power the kitchen so we can eat tonight, and a few other essentials."

Nathan furrowed his brow, his eyes darting about. "This isn't good. I don't like this."

Ellie rolled her eyes at him. "Afraid of the dark?"

Olwen frowned. "So the 'essentials' the generator is powering don't include the lights?" She hefted up her lantern.

Florence winced. "No, unfortunately, due to the size of Bulbrook Grove. However, everyone has a fireplace in their room, and we've already provided lots of candles." She plastered on a smile, almost pleading with Olwen to not push the issue. "I tried calling into town for the utility to send a technician, but the whole area's being hit pretty badly by the storm, and a lot of the roads are flooded. No one's able to get out to us."

Did she mean, *no one* could get here, or that the utility didn't have anyone available?

Janisa whimpered. "So we're... trapped here? In the dark?"

I had to admit, I didn't love that idea, either. Rain lashed against the wall of windows behind me, and with the heavy clouds, dusk had come early. Soon, the manor house would be cast in total darkness. While we'd gone low lights yesterday to sync our bodies' sleep rhythms to nature, that had been voluntary.

There was something unnerving about knowing we couldn't flip a light switch if we needed to. Plus, Irene had died last night, and who knew what Kurt would get up to, now that he suspected someone among us was a vampire doling out culty vitamin packets. Night around the manor house could be a dangerous time—especially in pitch blackness.

Bobby beamed at us, his dimples showing, clearly unfazed by his guests' trepidation. "But no reason for this to put a damper on our weekend, right?"

No one answered, but he continued on brightly. "This will make everything extra cozy. We'll get the fires going, we've got plenty of food and drink, and while it might get chilly without heat, we have plenty of extra blankets to curl up with."

Janisa sniffed and muttered under her breath, "So much for a luxury retreat."

Cho winked and announced to the room at large, "If anyone needs a cuddle buddy to help stay warm, I'm available."

"Thanks, buddy. I'll keep that in mind." Leo tried to slip an arm around Cho's shoulders, but his friend ducked away and scowled at him.

Ellie folded her arms across her dirty overalls. "If we really get put out or there's an emergency, the Land Rover can handle pretty high floodwaters."

Right. I'd seen the tall vehicle out in their garage. I relaxed a little, knowing we had a contingency plan, at least.

Bobby clapped his hands together. "Right, so... let's all settle in. Unfortunately, we'll be busy for the next few hours securing Bulbrook Grove against the storm. We'll have to put a pin in the rest of the activities for today."

I understood, of course, but experienced a brief pang of disappointment. I'd been looking forward to Bobby's cooking class on making Regency-era lemon custards.

He gave us an apologetic smile. "I also need a little more prep time, so we'll be pushing our dinner back a bit to seven o'clock. Enjoy some free time until then, and if you need anything, don't hesitate to flag one of us down." He gestured at himself, Florence, and Ellie.

Bzzzzzz.

I jumped as my phone vibrated in my pocket. I pulled it out and checked the caller ID.

I showed it up to Fitz. "Prescott."

He wasn't a fan of the detective inspector but he nodded, clearly as eager as I was to hear what the police had found out about Irene's death. I stepped away from the group to answer the call, stalking over toward the jacuzzi with the phone to my ear. "Hey. What's the word about Irene?"

Rain crashed in sheets against the windows as thunder rumbled outside.

"Hey, Minnie, can you grab Kurt?" Tension underlined Prescott's clipped words as a cacophony of phones ringing sounded in the background, along with loud chatter and shouts.

"Sure." I frowned. "Everything okay? Sounds pretty chaotic on your end."

He grunted. "It's been nonstop emergencies since the storm hit, and it's all hands on deck here at the station. I need to have a word with you two—and make sure you go somewhere private."

16

POISONED

"A word?" I turned my phone's screen so Kurt could see it was Prescott on the other end. The cold blue light highlighted the rough scars crisscrossing the hunter's chest—no doubt souvenirs of previous battles with vampires. How could Gus see those and not be afraid of getting romantically involved with him? Also, why he'd thrown his trench coat on, shirtless, over his wet swim trunks, I couldn't say—but it was a fashion choice.

Kurt squinted at the screen and nodded. "Excuse us," he called to the room at large. I followed him out of the pool area, guided by the orange light from his oil lantern.

"Prescott wants us to find somewhere private."

"Come on. I saw a good place over here earlier." Kurt jerked his head to the right, and we wound down a short hallway before ducking into a small, cozy study. Floor-to-ceiling bookshelves stuffed with leather tomes lined most of the room—I could've spent the whole weekend in here.

I pulled back the curtains on a tall window to let in what little soft gray light could be gained as Kurt pulled the heavy double doors shut behind us. He set the lantern on a polished end table between two wingback chairs, and we sat across from each other. The dark, intimate space did seem perfect for a secret talk.

I put my phone on speaker mode and set it between us next to the lantern. "Okay, Prescott, we're both here."

I leaned forward, and Kurt huddled closer. "What's the news?"

"Good." The hubbub sounded in the background as the detective inspector cleared his throat. "We got the preliminary findings back from the coroner."

My stomach clenched in the tense pause that followed, and Kurt gripped the arm of his chair.

"Irene Fernsby's blood contained high levels of amatoxins, phallotoxins, and virotoxins."

I raised my brows at Kurt—did he know what that meant? He shrugged at me, and I bent my face closer to the phone. "We're not sure the significance of that, but it doesn't sound good."

"It's not." Prescott lowered his voice. "What that means is, she was killed by poisonous mushrooms. Death cap mushrooms, to be specific."

I covered my mouth. "Like on the hike."

Kurt nodded at me. "Ellie Chang pointed out a large grouping of those very mushrooms here on the property, not too far from the house."

"They're actually fairly common, apparently," Prescott mused. "You were served mushrooms with dinner last night, correct?"

"Yeah." I pressed a hand to my stomach. "Are we in danger?"

"No, no, if you're not sick by now, you won't be. Nobody else has shown signs of poisoning? Headaches, nausea, disorientation?"

Kurt and I looked at each other. I shook my head, and he answered, "None."

Prescott made a thoughtful noise. "Our victim was likely targeted, then."

I bit my lip, still clinging to a shred of hope that that poor old lady hadn't been murdered. "Is there any chance Bobby served the deadly mushrooms on accident?"

"It's highly unlikely," Prescott answered. "We tested her stomach contents, and it was definitely something she ate at dinner and in large quantities. This wasn't a couple of errant mushrooms that snuck their way into the mix—someone served her a large dose of the poisonous variety, and *only* her by the sounds of it."

I nodded. That made sense. I didn't like it, but it made sense. "Bobby told me earlier that he picked the mushrooms himself. He was positive they weren't poisonous, and he's highly trained."

Kurt caught my eye and frowned. "And that just came up... organically?"

My face flushed warm. "Um... I *may* have questioned him a little bit."

Prescott huffed on the phone, though it sounded at least a little bit like maybe a disbelieving laugh. Kurt glowered at me, though. "You're cutting me out, Wells."

"Come on." I lifted a palm, feeling slightly guilty for not including him. "I doubt Irene's death has anything to do with vampires. I didn't see the need to, um, involve you."

Kurt sniffed and turned his head away. "You never know."

Why did I feel the urge to apologize to him? I didn't want to hurt Kurt's feelings, but I had to leave him out of some things. Otherwise, he might discover that I was a witch and almost all my friends had supernatural powers. So why did I genuinely feel remorseful for making the big guy feel overlooked?

"Don't be upset," I pleaded with the hunter.

"I'm not an expert, but I doubt vampires would resort to poisoned mushrooms."

Prescott had a point, which Kurt acknowledged with a shrug. He turned back to face me, which I interpreted as him forgiving me. Thank goodness. I couldn't handle having both Gus and him mad at me.

Prescott's voice, though a bit hoarse and weary, held a smile. "So, Minnie, since I know I can't keep you from investigating, what have you found?"

I grinned—he had me pegged. At least he didn't call it snooping like Gus did. "It turns out Bobby's having an affair with Florence, the business manager."

Kurt rolled his eyes. "That's obvious."

I nodded. "Yeah, but Irene caught them together out in the barn before the welcome tour yesterday. I saw it from my window."

The hunter stroked his stubbled chin. "So Bobby poisoned Irene to keep his affair a secret?"

"Maybe." I shrugged. "Only thing is, Bobby made a pretty compelling argument against that. He said he'd never do anything that might endanger his business. I guess he and Ellie have put everything they own, and then some, into this place. Killing someone—especially if they were poisoned by his cooking—could tank their wellness center before the end of the opening weekend."

"Hmm..." Kurt drummed his fingers on the leather chair arm.

"Plus," I continued. "Bobby admitted to cheating on Ellie back in London. She knew and still stayed with him. They came out here to Bath to start over. I tend to believe Bobby when he says he'd rather be caught having another affair than resort to murdering a poor old lady and destroying Bulbrook Grove in the process."

"Interesting." Some taps sounded on the other end—Prescott typing on his keyboard. "I'll do some digging around and confirm that the Changs are overleveraged on this business."

"Let us know what you find." I fidgeted with the hem of my jeans. "After I talked to Bobby, I suspected it might've been Janisa Davies, or her friend-slash-intern, Karine. I overheard Irene confronting them last night."

Kurt frowned. "Over what?"

"I guess Irene's husband died of lung cancer, which Janisa beat... or at least claimed to beat. It turns out she's been faking it for clout and Irene caught her in a lie."

Kurt pounded the chair of the arm. "Aha! Nice work, Minnie." He sobered. "Even though you should've included me."

I nodded. "Sorry." I winced. "But... it's not quite in the bag. I'm only *pretty* sure Janisa was faking."

"I'll check up on that, too," Prescott added.

"But Janisa seemed *entirely* unconcerned about Irene. She seemed to almost think it was a joke that Irene had threatened to expose her."

"She could've been lying." Kurt raised his brows.

I nodded. "Yeah, maybe, but I got the feeling it wasn't her. Janisa pointed out that Irene couldn't have worked social media if her life depended on it." I winced. "Sorry—bad choice of words. But also, who's to say anyone would believe some random old lady? Janisa has lots of avid followers ready to defend her." I shook my head. "I don't think she had enough motive for murder."

Prescott cleared his throat. "What's your current theory, then?"

I scrunched up my face. "I don't know. No one had even met Irene before this weekend, so who could want to kill some grumpy older lady they'd only known for a few hours? It's hard to imagine a compelling motive."

"I'll look into all the other guests and get back to you two if I find anything. Who knows. Maybe someone has a previous tie to our victim that we don't know about." He groaned. "I'd prefer to come down there immediately to collect evidence and do interviews, but with this storm and the roads flooded, I couldn't possibly get there. That's even *if* we had officers to spare. Everyone is needed to deal with all the issues the storm's causing, including me, so I won't be able to look into this more until later... probably tomorrow."

I whimpered. So we were definitely trapped at Bulbrook Grove with a killer—no one was getting in or out.

"We'll keep on it." Kurt nodded. "The murderer is bound to make a misstep, and when they do, we'll be ready to pounce and apprehend them."

I wish I shared his confidence. I only had a rising sense of panic at being stuck here in the dark.

"Hold tight, and don't do anything rash. Play it safe and make it through the night, got it?"

"Okay, yeah, we'll do that." Kurt winked at me, as if to say he'd for sure *not* be playing it safe.

"Irene was definitely killed by someone in that home," Prescott continued. "Be careful until the storm clears and we can get in—fingers crossed it'll be tomorrow morning."

We said our goodbyes and ended the call. I slumped forward in my chair, head in my hands and groaned. "Great, so we're confined here with Irene's killer, in the dark, with no way to access the police or outside world."

Kurt nodded. "*And* we've got a vampire among us—one I'm determined to root out."

"Oh, right." I let out a humorless chuckle. "How could I have forgotten about that?" The wellness weekend had officially turned into a nightmare.

17

BESTIES

Kurt flashed the rows of stakes lining his trench coat and excused himself with a wink to go do some "research." I took that to mean sniffing out the vitamin-packet vampire among us. The man was not subtle. My friends and I, including Gus, reconvened back in my and Fitz's room.

My bestie sat in one of the armchairs beside Yasmine, while Cho took up his spot at the desk chair, and Calvin squeezed in next to Leo and Al on the window seat. Fitz and I plopped down on the bed, while Dom leaned against the wall by the door, like a beefy bouncer.

With the orange light of the several lanterns and candles scattered about, it would've been snug and pleasant if it weren't for the murder and the violent rain lashing at the tall window.

I licked my lips. "Guys, that was DI Prescott on the phone. He confirmed that someone definitely murdered Irene by poisoning her with mushrooms."

Yasmine covered her mouth, and the news seemed to jolt even Calvin out of his moping. "No way."

I relayed what Kurt and I had discussed with the detective. "So, I don't think it was Bobby—he has too much to lose."

Fitz nodded, thoughtfully, with his big hands laced together over his knee. "That would presumably exclude Ellie, and possibly Florence from our suspect list as well, then?"

Yasmine folded her legs up under her. "Right, 'cause they wouldn't want to tank the opening weekend of the retreat... even if they had some reason to want to harm Irene."

"That poor old lady," Calvin muttered.

"So who does that leave?" Leo splayed his hands.

"Minnie and I talked to Janisa and Karine already. Janisa might've had a motive to silence Irene, but she seemed pretty flippant about the older woman airing her secret." Yasmine shrugged. "So that leaves Nathan, the travel writer, and Olwen, right? Plus, Kurt and Serena? Maybe they knew Irene before they got here?" She scrunched up her face. "But if that was the case, why act now?"

She raised some good questions.

Gus and I locked eyes for a moment before he rolled his and looked away, leaning his head elegantly in his hand. Ugh, I hated having tension between us.

Yasmine sat up straighter. "Okay, but what if the killer wasn't targeting Irene specifically? Like, maybe they wanted to sabotage the wellness center, and Irene was in the wrong place at the wrong time."

"Ooh." Cho's dark eyes widened, and he pointed at our witchy friend. "That's a creepy thought."

"Interesting," Fitz mused.

"Okay, let's follow that thought—why would someone want to ruin this place?" I shook my head. "No one seems to have met Bobby or Ellie before this weekend."

"And they'd have to be pretty cold to be willing to kill

some poor random old lady to tank this business," Leo added.

Calvin huffed. "So cold."

"Totally." I sighed. "I have a hard time seeing any of the guests being that ruthless."

"What about Serena?" The lantern in Leo's hands lit his curved nose and meticulously trimmed beard in sharp relief. "She is a vampire."

Cho made a face. "Nah, she seems nice."

Leo shot him a withering look. "You just think she's hot."

"She *is* hot!"

Yasmine and Al exchanged amused looks.

I darted a quick glance at Gus, nervous to bring up the hunter. "Kurt recognized that vitamin packet she gave you, Cho. He said it's part of a vampire cult, basically, that lures people into being turned and serving the head vamp."

Fitz turned his dark gaze to me. "Darius?"

I grimaced. "I don't know for sure. He didn't have a name, but... it sounds like him, doesn't it?"

My boyfriend rubbed his hands together and breathed heavily, clearly upset about the turn this had taken. I didn't blame him. He'd been forced into Darius's clutches as an indentured servant for decades. I was sure it was upsetting to know he was still up to his old tricks, only with new tactics.

"But why would Serena kill that lady?" Cho drummed on the back of the chair. "Not to like, stereotype or whatever"—he shot a nervous glance at Gus—"but don't vampires usually bite their victims?"

My stylish friend acknowledged the point with a lift of his blond brows.

"Plus, if she's got this gig, teaching yoga and recruiting for the cult, wouldn't she want to fly under the radar?" Yasmine fidgeted with the hem of her loose comfy pants. "You'd think she'd *avoid* killing people."

"So who else could've killed Irene?" Leo raised a sculpted brow.

Cho shrugged. "Kurt?"

I scoffed. "No."

Leo flashed his eyes at me. "Wow. Really defending your vampire hunter buddy, huh?"

I squirmed, crossing my legs under me. "He's not my buddy." I shot him a dismissive look, but as I thought about it, my confidence faded. We shared memes and texts almost daily, he had saved my life a few months ago, and I *had* felt guilty leaving him out of the loop earlier. I covered my mouth. "Oh my—" My breath caught and I turned wide-eyed to Fitz. "Kurt is kinda my buddy." I gasped, slightly horrified. When did that happen?

"You sure? You seem pretty convinced he's dangerous." Gus kept his tone light, but an oily bite lay below his words. He shot me a pointed look.

Were we really going to hash this out in front of everyone? I tried to play it cool and hugged a pillow to my stomach. "Well, he *is* a vampire hunter. I think that warrants some caution." I shot him a pointed look back. "But I guess some of us don't have the same sense of self-preservation the rest of us do."

The crackle and pop of the fire filled the tense silence. Fitz slowly reached over and gently took my hand.

"Uh..." Cho let out a nervous chuckle. "Are you guys like... fighting?"

"No," Gus answered, at the same time I said, "Yes."

We glared at each other.

"Hoo," Al breathed out.

"How are we not fighting? We're fighting." I threw my hands up.

Cho cringed. "So now you're fighting about whether or not you're fighting?"

"Guys!" Calvin stretched his arms out, as if to hold us

back from each other. Everyone's attention swung to the youngest butler, who'd been uncharacteristically downcast and quiet the last couple of days. "Don't fight, you guys." He looked imploringly between Gus and me. "Especially over lovers."

Gus curled his lip at the term, and I shot a questioning look at the young guy.

He shook his head. "Boyfriends come and go, okay? But friends don't leave you when they find a taller friend." He dropped his gaze, half speaking to himself. "Who has a car."

Yikes. This sounded like it was more about Rachel than Gus and me. Al rubbed Calvin's back and muttered some support as he buried his head in his hands.

Gus shook it off and turned back to me. He tipped his head, almost looking bored, which was more infuriating than if he'd been visibly upset with me. "We're not fighting. Minnie is expressing her upset that I've gotten involved with Kurt Alpenjager."

There were a few surprised murmurs from around the room, and Yasmine's dark eyes grew wide. "Really?"

"Whoa, man." Leo shook his head. "As a supernatural? I gotta say, that's playing with fire."

"Thank you." I shook my head at Gus. "I'm not upset because I have something personally against Kurt—I'm upset that you're putting yourself at risk."

He raised his brows. "Now you know how I felt when you were first getting involved with your ex, Desmond."

I gasped. "Seriously?" That was a low blow, to bring up my loser, cheating ex-husband.

But Gus pressed on. "Would you have stopped seeing him if I told you my opinion of him? That he didn't deserve you. That you were in danger of having your heart broken and youth wasted. Would that have changed your path?"

I puffed up my chest but found I couldn't deny it like I wanted to. Back then, in college, I'd viewed the very British, handsome Desmond as something of my prince charming. He was popular on campus, and I didn't have the self-esteem to see that he treated me pretty terribly. At the time, I thought I was lucky to have been chosen by him, and happily molded my life to fit his. I'd learned and grown a lot since then, but old Minnie...?

I sighed, my stomach tight. "Well, no, probably not." I opened my mouth to qualify my answer, but Gus continued in clipped tones.

"I also have a few centuries on you, and a lot more romantic experience." A small grin tugged at the corner of his lips. "And yet, despite my many years and all I've experienced, I find Kurt refreshingly new and intriguing."

I shook my head. "He'll be new and intriguing until he stakes you."

My friend tipped his head, his expression softening. "Minnie, do you know how rare it is for someone as old as I am to feel something novel? I don't deny that what I'm pursuing has its risks, but what's the point of living if not to truly feel? I'm not ready to let go of it."

Everyone else swiveled their gazes to me.

"That's actually kind of sweet."

I shot Leo a "nobody asked you" look.

Gus leaned toward me. "Minnie, you have a big heart, and I know you care deeply about me and your other friends here." He gestured around the room. "But sometimes, you need to let go and trust that others can take care of themselves."

I sucked in a deep breath. While the tightness in my chest released a bit, my stomach still churned with unease. I addressed the room. "You guys feel like I trust you, right?"

Leo smirked. "Mostly, yeah, but you have to admit you have some trust issues in general."

I gaped at him. "What?"

"I love you for your determination and how deeply you

care for those around you." Fitz gently squeezed my hand. "But the other side of that coin is that at times..." He pressed his lips together. "You might stray toward being a tad over-invested."

He might be right, but I didn't have to admit it. "Traitor." I squeezed his hand back.

"Usually that is for the best." Al winked. "Like when you got us all to share about our unique abilities."

"And the way you all but forced me to hire you and rebrand the tearoom," Fitz added with a smile. "Best decision I was ever obliged to make."

I chuckled. "Okay, you have some points."

Yasmine shot me a soft grin. "And when was the last time you actually stepped back and allowed the police to solve a crime?"

I clicked my tongue. "Well, come on, sometimes I do a better job." Gus raised a brow, and I slumped lower behind my pillow. "Argh, alright, I guess yes, that's me thinking I know better."

Fitz rubbed his thumb across the back of my hand. I sighed at Gus. "I'm sorry, Gus. I still don't like it, but okay. I'll stay out of your relationship with Kurt and respect your decisions. I—I should trust you more."

Gus smirked at me from under his blond lashes. "I forgive you."

"Aw." Cho beamed at us. "You guys made up."

I rolled my shoulders. "This is still going to take some getting used to. And how will this ever end well? And what if—" I snapped my mouth shut and blew out a breath through my nose, stopping myself. "Sorry. I'm letting it go."

Gus chuckled. "I'm a big vampire, Minnie, I can take care of myself." His gaze softened. "But thank you for caring."

I gave him a wry smile. "I obviously can't help it." I couldn't say I was totally alright with this situation, but the tension had lifted, and it felt good to be playful and easy with Gus again.

Dom, who leaned against the wall, shook his head. "Change of subject: we still have no idea who the killer is."

Oh, yeah. That. I wished we could review security tapes or something from dinner the other night to see if anyone slipped poisonous mushrooms onto Irene's plate. I doubted Bobby and Ellie had installed security cameras, but it gave me another idea.

I sat up straighter. "Janisa and Karine have been taking a million pics since we got here yesterday, right?"

Yasmine chuckled. "At least that many."

I opened my phone and found Janisa's social media accounts. "Maybe she caught some clue on camera."

Fitz looked over my shoulder. "Intriguing idea."

"I'll look, too," Cho chimed in, grabbing his phone from his pocket.

A few of the others followed suit and we scrolled for a few minutes in silence. Most of Janisa's pictures featured flowers or stone walls in the background, or had been taken in her room at the window seat. She'd been careful to keep anyone else out of the background. I was losing hope of finding anything unusual until I stumbled on a photo from last night's dinner.

"Hold up!"

18

TARGETED

I frowned down at the picture on my phone. In it, Janisa pouted at the camera with a flute of champagne in her hand and the flames burning in the elegant fireplace behind her. The angle caught a peek of the others near her. Karine had taken the picture from one side of Janisa and Florence sat on her other side, right behind her in the photo.

Something nagged at me. I tilted my head, trying to puzzle out what was off. That missing piece slid into place. Why had we all thought Janisa might've killed Irene if she wasn't sitting anywhere near her? Except...

I showed the photo to Yasmine. "In the locker room—you said Janisa sat right next to Irene at dinner."

Cho nodded. "She did."

"But look—" I pinched the picture to enlarge it and pointed at Florence. "In this photo, Florence is sitting beside her, not Irene."

Cho scrunched up his face. "Oh yeah, Irene switched places with Florence because she was cold or something."

I gasped. "That's right—I remember her complaining about the drafts." I checked the photo again. Karine had also captured the plate of steaming chicken and mushrooms on the table in front of Janisa. "They have their food in front of them, here. Cho, did Irene carry her plate with her when she got up?"

His gaze grew far away as he cast back in his memory. "No—I don't think so."

Yasmine nodded her agreement. "I remember—they definitely left their plates in place on the table, and only switched seats."

Chills crept down my spine and goose bumps rose on my arms. "This changes everything. What if Irene wasn't the intended victim? What if it was *Florence,* and when she and Irene switched places, Irene ended up eating the poisoned mushrooms intended for the retreat's manager?"

"Whoa," Cho breathed.

Calvin shook his head. "Poor Irene."

We all sat in stunned silence, the only sounds coming from the crackling fire and the whooshing wind and rain outside.

"Who would want Florence dead?" Leo mused.

"Ellie, obviously," Dom offered.

Yasmine bit her lip. "*If* she knew about the affair."

"They're not the best at hiding it." Leo flashed his eyes.

I couldn't disagree. "But why now? Bobby cheated on Ellie in London, and they stayed together and even moved here for a new start. Plus, a murder might sabotage the wellness center, which she's just as invested in as Bobby is." I frowned and fidgeted with my phone. "Seems strange that she'd attack *now*, of all times."

Fitz nodded. "But she did serve the food from the kitchen, so she had access to the plate."

"And she obviously knows a lot about poisonous mushrooms," Yasmine added. "She's the one who led the hike and made sure to point them out to us."

I nodded. We probably should look into Ellie Chang.

She was the most obvious person who'd want Florence dead, since the manager was cheating with her husband. But who else might hold a grudge against the retreat manager?

"Ahhhhh!"

A bloodcurdling scream sent my stomach into my throat. I jumped and lurched to my feet, as did my friends. Dom was already out the door, and we poured into the hall after him, lanterns raised. My heart pounded quicker as another scream sounded.

"It came from the right."

"It sounded like Janisa."

Our group surged down the hall and banged on Janisa's door. A moment later, Karine threw the door open and blinked at us, wide-eyed and breathless. "Help."

Behind her, Janisa cringed on the floor, a pillow hugged to her chest as she gaped at the flickering shadows on the wall above their two canopied beds. She pointed a trembling finger in that direction, and Dom, Fitz, and Gus rushed forward, looking under the beds and then checking the bathroom.

I dashed to Janisa's side and crouched beside her, with Cho and Leo right behind me. "Are you okay? What happened?"

The candles and firelight cast stark shadows on her face and around the room. She blinked at us, her pupils huge. "It—it was this giant crab." She spread her arms wide. "And it told me that I was the queen of the crab people. Which..." She started to cry. "I don't want to be a crab person."

Leo, Cho, and I exchanged confused looks. I turned to Karine, who thrust a hand at her friend. "She started screaming and saying gibberish."

I shook my head. "What's wrong with her? Could she have been poisoned, too?"

Karine rolled her eyes. "Nah. She ate the magic mushroom in the locker room, remember?"

I pressed a hand to my racing heart, torn between relief and annoyance that they'd scared me half to death. "Oh, right."

Yasmine shot me an exasperated look as Karine stood beside her friend and stroked Janisa's hair.

"Did you two make up?" Last time I'd seen them, they hadn't been able to be on the same side of the pool together.

The brunette rolled her eyes. "I mean, I'm probably still going to expose her for being a fake, but..." She grimaced around the shadowy, dark room. "It's spooky, and we gotta stick together for now."

We all filed back into the hall after making sure Karine had the situation under control. Rain lashed against the big windows, and thunder rumbled ominously overhead. The flickering orange light from the oil lanterns cast spooky shadows over the various busts and paintings lining the wide hallway.

We huddled up and Yas asked, "What now?"

I nibbled my lip. "Okay, Kurt's off investigating Serena." I turned to Gus. "Could you and maybe a few others go find him and make sure he doesn't do anything... er... stake-y?"

My blond friend gave me a wry smile but nodded. "If it will ease your mind."

I flashed my eyes. "It would. And please don't go alone, for safety's sake."

"Fine."

Cho nudged Leo. "We'll go along, too."

I nodded. "The rest of us can split up in small groups and poke around. Let's talk to the others and see if we can figure out why one of them might've wanted Florence dead?"

Everyone agreed to meet back up in our room in half an hour.

We all split up, with Fitz and I sticking together. "I was thinking—when we first got here, it sounded like Ellie and Florence were arguing about something, remember?"

"That's right." Fitz narrowed his eyes. "Something about 'greasing the wheels,' if I recall correctly?"

I nodded. "Right—let's head back toward the foyer. I think Ellie or Florence's office must be right off it."

We moved slowly together, the halls eerily dark, with only the low light of one of the oil lanterns to light our way. Of course, being a vampire, Fitz was used to the dark. He'd have been fine without any light at all, but I'd have been blind, so he gallantly held the lamp aloft for me.

We threaded our way around the shadows of furniture in the lounge, then returned to the foyer. I pointed to the left. "Let's try that way."

Fitz and I crept down the carpeted runner and stepped up to the first door. I tried the crystal knob, found it unlocked, and pushed it open.

Light from Fitz's lantern flooded the room, illuminating a wide-eyed Olwen standing behind a heavy wooden desk. We all froze. She held her phone up as a flashlight in one hand, with a stack of papers in the other. The rest of the room, with its dark fireplace, two silk armchairs, and built-in bookcases, sat empty and quiet.

"What are you—?"

"Oops." The mommy blogger's cheeks flushed bright pink as she dropped the papers and slammed the desk drawer shut. She skirted the desk and dashed toward us. "My bad—I got lost in the dark."

That made no sense. Fitz and I stepped aside as she slid past and hurried off down the hall, disappearing around the corner before we had a chance to respond.

Fitz and I exchanged shocked looks.

"What was that?"

He sucked in a breath and shook his head, as though he had no words.

We hesitated at the threshold, suddenly unsure about snooping around now that we'd caught Olwen doing the same. "Whatever that was, it was weird." I leaned forward, peering into the cozy space. "Whose office is this?"

No photos on the wall or name plate on the desk made it obvious.

"It's certainly not Olwen's."

I turned to Fitz. "True. What was she doing in here?" I scrunched up my face. "She's a family blogger, right? Sounds pretty innocent. Why in the world would she be snooping?"

Fitz fought a grin. "You mean sleuthing?"

I tried not to laugh. "It's only sleuthing when I do it."

"What's going on?"

We both turned toward the raised voice. Ellie marched toward us, her lantern held high, jaw set. Her gaze darted between the office door, now ajar, and us. She slammed it shut, pulled some keys out of her pocket, and locked the door, then rounded on Fitz and me. "What were you doing in there?"

We exchanged nervous looks, and Fitz took the lead. "We did not actually enter. We were looking for you, though, and found the door ajar."

Nicely done, Fitz. I thought it was probably wise to leave Olwen out of this, at least until we had more information.

Ellie narrowed her eyes, staring us each down for a long moment as if she thought she might catch us in a lie, before finally relenting. She sighed and crossed her arms. "Well, I can tell you I didn't leave it that way."

"How odd," Fitz murmured.

She sighed, as if resigned that she wouldn't get any more information out of us. "Well, you found me. What did you need?"

Fitz and I exchanged looks. We'd hoped to snoop around her office without running into her. But now that we had her, how to best ask if she'd attempted to kill Florence as revenge for the affair with her husband? If anyone could approach the subject with tact it'd be Fitz.

He gave the impatient Ellie a slight bow of his head. "Erm, at our Bath Butler Cafe, we pride ourselves on our courtesy and decorum."

"Mm-hmm." Ellie urged him to get on with it.

"Which can at times be a challenge to maintain, considering our mostly female demographic is often drawn to the business by the charms of our butlers."

Ellie frowned, clearly as confused as I was about where Fitz was going with this.

He cleared his throat. "What I'm driving at, I suppose, is that it can be difficult to sustain professionalism when the boundaries between business and the personal are pushed. However, that is of utmost importance, and Minnie and I need to be assured that if we were to recommend Bulbrook Grove to our customers, they would experience the same level of propriety and respectability here."

"Oh." Ellie waved it off. "Please understand, this is a freak storm, and I doubt we'll see weather like this often. Now that we know it can happen, though, I'll talk to Bobby about getting more powerful backup generators so future guests won't be inconvenienced like this."

Fitz licked his lips and laced his hands behind his back. "Of course, we understand this."

I nodded along.

"However, I was referring to a more, er, delicate matter. We noticed some—forgive me—*closeness* between your husband and your manager, Florence. We were unsure if you were aware of their quite friendly relationship or..."

Ellie squeezed her eyes shut, and even in the dim light of

the lantern, her face turned visibly red. She blew out a heavy breath and set her jaw. "Yes, yes, I am aware."

Even though Fitz had danced around the topic in his polite way, she'd clearly gotten the message. Interesting. She knew about their affair, or at least their flirting, and it clearly bothered her.

Her nostrils flared as she lifted her chin. "I'll be sure to speak to Bobby about being more discreet so as not to make our guests uncomfortable or confused."

I held up a palm. "Wait—if you know about them, does that mean you're okay with it?"

She shrugged, a tense, jerky movement. "I don't love it, no, and thank you *so much* for bringing up this super pleasant topic for me."

I grimaced in apology.

"Of course it bothers me, but..." She huffed. "That's Bobby. He's always been like this, and at the end of the day, I'm his wife, and I'm the one he chooses to come back to. The other women are mere distractions that come and go—I know that, he knows it." She turned to Fitz. "And I'll make sure they keep a lid on it, so the guests don't need to know about it."

She stuck her hands in her overall pockets. "Anything else?" She barely waited a beat before muttering, "Great. If you'll excuse me, I've got to go look after the animals." She double-checked that the office door was locked, and then stomped off down the hall.

We waited until she rounded the corner to speak.

"What do you think about that?" I asked Fitz.

He narrowed his eyes. "I could hear her heart rate—it was elevated. She was more agitated by the questions than she was letting on, but she didn't seem surprised by the news of the affair."

I shook my head. "No. And that thing she said about

Bobby always being like this lined up with what he told us himself about his affair in London."

"So, the only motive I can think of for Ellie to attempt to kill Florence would be revenge over the affair." I shrugged. "And she seems, if not approving of it, at least accepting of it." I shook my head. "I don't think Ellie's our gal."

Fitz slid his hand into mine and held the lantern aloft. We stepped down the hall toward the lounge. "If Florence was indeed the murderer's intended target, then who besides Ellie would have wanted to kill her?"

I bit my lip. "That's the big question, isn't it?" Plus, what had Olwen been up to in Ellie's office?

19

SCRYING TOGETHER

Between the fire crackling in the fireplace, the dozen candles flickering around the room, the oil lanterns, and the light from my laptop screen, I could see tolerably well. I jumped at a particularly startling crack of thunder and tried to shake off the creeps.

With my phone functioning as a hotspot—since the power had been knocked out—I opened the internet browser. "It has to be one of us here in the house, right? I'm going to look into the other guests some more."

A knock at the door sounded, and Fitz let Dom, Leo, Al, and Yasmine back in. Gradually, the others trickled back, until all my friends crowded inside. Unfortunately, nobody had learned anything useful during their sweeps of the house. On the plus side, though, Gus reported that Kurt had vowed he was going to take a nap.

"At least we don't have to worry about him going all 'stake-y,' as you put it, on Serena." Gus raised a blond brow in amusement, and I shot him a challenging look.

"Or so he says."

But Kurt was the least of my worries for now. I looked around at my friends. "So we're trapped in here with an unknown killer, who might've been targeting Irene or Florence, for a mysterious motive." The hairs rose on the back of my neck. "Personally, I'm not going to feel safe until we figure out who killed Irene."

Fitz clasped his big hands together over his knee. "We did discover Olwen rummaging through Ellie's desk."

Cho nodded. "That's definitely shady." He sat backwards in the desk chair—what I now thought of as his spot.

"And a good place to start..." I found Olwen's mommy blog online, something she called "The Farm Fresh Family." I scrolled through beautiful pictures of healthy meals, Olwen cooking in her kitchen with her children nearby, and occasional shots of a garden or Olwen foraging in nature. That jogged my memory.

"You know, I did see something odd this morning. Olwen pretended to tie her shoelace on our hike, but she actually pocketed something near those poisonous mushrooms."

Leo gawked at me. "Uh... as in, she definitely collected some poisonous mushrooms?"

"Yeah, I think so. But that doesn't mean she poisoned anyone the day before, right?" I continued to scroll through her blog. "If she already had some death caps, why collect more?"

Leo perched on the window seat with Calvin and Al and spread his palms wide. "Uh, obviously because she plans to poison someone else." He grimaced. "Or all of us."

Calvin shuddered. "That's creepy."

"Super creepy." I searched Olwen's site for any sign that she might be a killer. After a few minutes, I sighed. "I don't know, guys, she looks like a normal blogger. She writes about cooking, family stuff, farm fresh food." I clicked over to her bio and scanned it. "It says she grew up on a local farm, but doesn't specify which one." I shrugged. "It's pretty typical stuff."

"Keep looking," Leo urged. "You never know."

I scrolled and scrolled, skimming through years' worth of blog entries until I stumbled on pictures from her wedding. I studied the photos, but didn't spot anyone familiar. As I read her post though, a short recap of her big day, something jumped out at me, though I couldn't say why. "She changed her maiden name, Feldman, and took her husband's last name, Combestock." I drummed my fingers on my keyboard without typing. "Feldman... why does that name sound familiar?"

I kept searching, and after reaching the very first blog entry, the end of the line, I closed my laptop. I scrubbed my achy eyes and groaned. "Nothing there, and I need a break. I'm getting a headache."

Yas lifted a palm. "I'll look into Nathan." She pulled out her phone.

Cho scoffed. "Seriously, guys?" He gestured around the room. "We've got a bunch of supernatural folks here—there's got to be something super you can do to figure this out." He wiggled his fingers like he was casting a spell, and I grinned. He was being a bit ridiculous, but he had a point.

I turned to Dom. "You saw Irene's ghost this morning—have you tried talking to her since then?" He'd been able to speak with an even older ghost a few months ago, and together we'd figured out who killed her.

But the big guy shook his head, looking poutier than ever. "I think she passed over."

Good for Irene's spirit, but not too helpful for us.

I bit my lip and gestured at our resident shifter, Leo. "Maybe you could, like, shift and eavesdrop or something?"

He snorted out a laugh. "It's kind of hard to blend in as a lion."

Dur. I mentally smacked my forehead. For some reason, I'd been thinking he could sneak around outside, and use his feline prowess to quietly listen in or spy on our suspects.

But no one was going outside in this downpour, except for Ellie to check on the horses and chickens. And I was certain an enormous lion would spook the animals, even if he managed to go unseen by Ellie.

Fitz lifted a palm. "It's a good idea, though. Gus or I could change into bat form and spy."

My stomach turned, and I immediately regretted even suggesting it to Leo. "No." I shook my head. "I've seen you two in bat form. You're huge, and Kurt would immediately know you were vampires. That's way too dangerous."

I half expected some pushback from Gus, since I knew I was being a little overprotective of my friends, but thankfully he smirked and nodded his agreement. He was definitely letting me have a pass here.

Yas raised her brows at me. "Guess that leaves us and our witchy powers." She wiggled her fingers like Cho had and giggled.

I nodded. "Okay. You know, I've divined clues in the past. We could try that?"

She pushed to her feet. "Ooh, fun. I haven't divined with anyone in forever."

I slid off the bed. "I've only scried by myself."

"It'll be great," she gushed, looking around the room. "I think the best place to do it would be here." She gestured at the open space on the rug in front of the fire, then turned to Al. "Will you grab us some candles?"

I rummaged around in my luggage and retrieved my tools—the black-lined bowl, crystals, and feather I'd brought along, just in case. Maybe some part of me had anticipated the restful weekend turning into something a little more mysterious, after all.

Yasmine and I lowered ourselves onto the rug, sitting criss-cross on top of some throw pillows. The dark bowl full of water sat between us, surrounded by flickering candles and glittering crystals. I placed the feather horizontally in front of me and gave Yas an awkward smile. The guys all sat around us, watching curiously.

"I've never had an audience before."

She smirked. "Me, neither." She reached out and took my hands in her own warm ones. "Pretend they're not there."

"Cho should be used to that from women," Leo quipped.

They proceeded to bicker, and I barked, "Hey!"

They turned to me wide-eyed and immediately stopped talking.

"We're doing some witchcraft here."

They murmured apologies and, chastened, lowered their eyes. I turned back to Yasmine, who was fighting not to laugh. I winked at her and then closed my eyes.

"Okay, what next?"

"Do whatever you typically do when you're scrying, and I'll focus on boosting your power."

"Alright, I can do that." I sucked in a shaky breath, then blew it out slowly. Yas squeezed my hands and I started by thinking about my breath—inhaling, and exhaling. Gradually, my shoulders relaxed, and I breathed more deeply. With the goal of being present and tapping into my power, I focused next on the sounds in the room.

As my attention grew sharper, the crackle and pop of the fire seemed louder, as did the gutter of the candles, Yas's breathing, and the whoosh of the wind and rain outside. I even detected the quiet rush of the river down below, swollen with the storm and fueling my powers.

My fingertips tingled, and I decided to incorporate Serena's meditation technique from class the night before. Just because she was possibly in a vampire cult didn't mean she didn't know her stuff when it came to mindfulness.

I labeled every thought and emotion that entered my brain. Without even trying, the outside world dropped away.

I floated through infinite space, anchored to the physical only by my breath and Yasmine's warm hands.

I set my intention. *Ether, give me clarity about Olwen.*

A series of images flickered through my mind. Irene eating the mushroom chicken at dinner. Olwen rummaging through the desk papers. Ellie chastising Florence for "greasing the wheels." Digging in the dark soil of the garden. Bumping along the winding road up to the retreat and passing the foreclosed farm sign.

"That's it!" I opened my eyes, and the candles all extinguished at once, as if they'd been blown out at the exact same moment.

"Yikes!" Cho leapt into a crouch on the chair, looking wildly around.

Smoke curled away from the candles as I grinned at Yas, who looked a bit startled. I squeezed her hands before letting them go. "Sorry. I got excited."

"That was quick."

I nodded. "It normally takes me a lot longer. That was great, working together—your magic totally gave me a boost."

My witch friend smiled wider and rolled her wrist as she bowed her head. "Happy to be of assistance."

Fitz helped me to my feet as Al handed Yas up off the floor. My boyfriend smiled at me. "Well done, Minnie."

"Well, don't leave us hanging," Leo groused. "What did you learn?"

I held up my palms and turned to Gus and Fitz. "Do you guys remember passing that foreclosed farm sign on the way here, yesterday? It was on the last stretch, right before we climbed the hill?"

Gus shrugged, and Fitz frowned, casting back in his memory, but shook his head. I turned to the others. "Anyone?"

Yas screwed up her face. "Vaguely."

I waved my hands. "Doesn't matter. There was a big sign for a farm but, like I said, it had a "foreclosed" notice on it. It was the Feldman Farm." I raised my brows waiting for the recognition to dawn on everyone's faces.

Dom merely frowned. "And?"

"And, Olwen's maiden name was Feldman." I beamed at Fitz. "I knew it rang a bell."

Calvin frowned. "That's odd."

I nodded. "More than odd. Her bio said she grew up on a local farm—stands to reason it might be the Feldman Farm, right?"

Al helped Yas back into the armchair beside Gus. My friend nibbled her full bottom lip. "If so, that makes Olwen's family farm neighbors with the Bulbrook Grove estate, right?"

"Her *foreclosed* family farm," Cho added.

Gus steepled his fingers. "Intriguing."

I paced in front of the fireplace, careful not to overturn the candles and scrying bowl on the rug.

"Based on her blog posts, foraging isn't something new for Olwen." Leo folded his beefy arms. "She'd have known where to find death cap mushrooms in the wild even before this morning."

"And we caught her snooping in Ellie's office," Fitz added.

I kept pacing. We were right on the edge of piecing all the little bits of evidence together. I just couldn't quite see how it all fit, yet. "But why would Olwen want to kill Florence? Or possibly Irene?"

Gus splayed a long-fingered hand. "Perhaps Bulbrook Grove hasn't been a good neighbor."

Interesting thought. "Could they have something to do with the farm closing down?"

Al scrunched up his face as he stood behind Yas,

rubbing her shoulders. "But wouldn't she have wanted to kill Ellie or Bobby, the owners, instead of Florence?"

I stopped dead. "Unless she wasn't targeting anyone in particular. What if she wanted to get revenge on *Bulbrook Grove*—shut the place down by ruining its reputation?"

Cho gave an exaggerated shudder. "Oof. Spooky thought."

"Looks like someone will need to have a little talk with Olwen," Gus said, arching a brow.

He was right. But I wanted to make sure it was a fruitful conversation, one we could trust. I turned to Yas. "Are you up for a little more witchy magic?"

She grinned. "Always. What do you have in mind?"

"I want to brew a truth serum. Think we can pull it off?"

We figured out we'd brought most of the needed ingredients between the two of us, and Cho, Leo, and Dom were able to steal the rest (a smattering of herbs) from the kitchen. While we didn't have a cauldron—the ideal witchy vessel—we made do with a dutch oven (also borrowed from our hosts without their knowledge) that we rigged up in our fireplace.

An hour later, with the sun fully set and the manor in deep shadows, we'd brewed a passable truth serum. It'd been so much easier with Yasmine's help, and I was beginning to understand why our mentor Mim had been urging me to join up with a coven. It helped to have witchy sisters—plus it made magic more fun. I eyed the fizzy lilac liquid we'd poured into Leo's glass water bottle. "It looks right."

Yas waggled her dark brows. "Only one way to find out if it works."

Cho and Calvin marveled at the potion, then at Yas and me. "Okay, that was pretty impressive."

Calvin looked awestruck. "Can you make a potion for a broken heart?"

Yas and I shared a sympathetic look, then turned to

Calvin. "We'll talk to Mim, okay? Maybe she can whip something up for you." Poor guy. After we found our killer and, fingers crossed, survived a night in the spooky manor, I'd work on helping boost his spirits... and maybe cast a little teensy hex on his ex.

20

ALONE IN THE DARK

The sun fully set, and the dark, shadowy manor gave off a truly eerie ambience. With only soft flames and flashes of lightning to see by, no one had the urge to split up. As a tight group, me, Fitz, Yasmine, Gus, and the butlers crept down the wide hallway in search of Olwen. I patted the pocket of my cardigan, double checking that the little vial of truth serum—still warm from being brewed—was safe.

"Ol-wen? Oll-wennnn?"

Leo scowled at Cho. "It sounds like you're calling for a pet."

His quip got a small laugh out of me, despite my trepidation.

No one answered. It seemed the retreat's activity schedule had gone out the window as Florence, Ellie, and Bobby scrambled to keep the generator working, take care of the farm animals, and do everything else needed to secure the old building against the torrential downpour outside.

I peeked through a tall window, down the lawn, at the

swollen river. It churned, water lapping over the banks, threatening to flood the grassy yard and garden. At least the house itself was set up high on a hill. We edged past a spooky bust, my heart beating against my chest. Wherever the other guests were, they weren't in the study, pool room, gym, or central lounge.

"Everyone's probably hunkered down in their rooms, right?" Al shot Yasmine a nervous look, their hands intertwined as he gently supported her. She'd been experiencing a bout of good health this weekend, but casting the spell to brew the potion had taken it out of her, and she now leaned on her husband.

Gus sniffed. "I sensed a couple of heartbeats behind the door of those two girls." Janisa and Karine were probably still riding the influencer's mushroom trip out in their shared room.

Calvin shot my bestie a wide-eyed look and shook his head, as though he couldn't believe that Gus could actually hear their heartbeats. I didn't blame him. He'd only learned about the supernatural world a few months ago. It took me at least that long to come to terms with it.

Leo, Fitz, and Dom held lanterns aloft for our group. We pushed through the door into the dining room with its long table, and dark, empty seats. Without the crackle of the fire, or happy chatter, the eerie silence sent a shiver down my spine.

I scanned the room. "Maybe the kitchen? But guests aren't supposed to go in—ahh!" I shrieked as a beam of orange lantern light fell on a figure sitting at the far end of the table. Out of pure instinct, I skittered backward. Fitz caught me before I backpedaled over everyone else and retreated out the door.

Olwen lifted a hand and squinted, shielding her eyes from the multiple lanterns now held out toward her. "Oof, mind lowering those a bit?"

Fitz held firmly onto my shoulders as I fought to catch my breath, my heart still pounding with adrenaline. "What are you doing in here, in the dark, by yourself?" I gasped.

"That's straight up killer behavior, if you ask me," Leo muttered out of the corner of his mouth.

Cho raised a brow and nodded his assent.

As I panted, still half-terrified, I had to agree. I edged closer with the group until I could better see our fellow guest. A notebook sat in front of her, which she pressed closed with one hand, as though to keep its contents hidden from us. A near empty cup of tea steamed beside her, along with her phone, a pen, a smoking taper candle in a holder, and a small, narrow glass jar with something dark inside.

The mommy blogger followed my gaze to the glass and snatched it up, stashing it in her fanny pack before I could get a better look. Still, I'd seen enough to be fairly sure it was the vial that contained the poisonous mushrooms she'd collected on our hike. Was she in the middle of plotting to kill again?

"So..." She raised her brows at us like she was a bit put out by our interruption. "What's up, guys?"

I supposed it would feel strange to have the nine of us standing over her, staring. I shot Yasmine a significant look, then darted my eyes to her teacup. She seemed to pick up on my hint to create a distraction and moved to Olwen's other side, with Al assisting her. "We were looking for everyone else. What are you up to? Were you sitting here in the dark?" My friend gave an exaggerated shudder. "Little creepy, isn't it? This place gives me the willies."

Olwen narrowed her eyes but spun in her chair to answer Yasmine. As soon as her back was turned, I uncorked the vial of truth serum and tipped the bubbling contents into what remained of her tea. Hopefully, she wouldn't notice the much higher waterline.

"Um, no." Olwen gestured at the smoking candle. "I was

working by candlelight, but heard you all coming." She frowned. "Of course, I didn't know it was you lot. I thought it might be Bobby, Ellie, and Florence, and I didn't want them to catch me with this." She spun around again and picked up her steaming mug of tea. "I know we're not supposed to go into the kitchen, but you're right. It's a bit eerie in here, and I needed some tea to calm my nerves. I couldn't bloody find anyone, so I helped myself. Anyway, I wasn't in the mood to be scolded about it, so I extinguished the light, hoping I'd go unnoticed in case you all were the owners or Florence." She sipped from her tea, as if to demonstrate that had been her main motive for behaving secretively.

Yasmine caught my eye and raised a questioning brow. I nodded to indicate I'd added the potion, and a smile tugged at the corner of her lips. Mission partly accomplished. I crossed my fingers that the potion would work. Magic wasn't always predictable and didn't affect everyone the same way. It might kick in right away to prompt truthfulness from Olwen, it might never work, or it might be at its strongest at midnight tonight when it would do us no good. Time to test it.

Gus peeked over the middle-aged lady's shoulder, her wavy hair pulled back into a low ponytail. "By the by, what *are* you working on?"

She leaned forward, covering the notebook with her folded arm, then took another sip of her tea. "Oh, some personal research... er... for my blog."

I slid into the seat on her right side. She pressed her lips together and scooted forward, as if ready to pack her stuff up and bolt. "Cool. Do you think you're going to write about the power outage?"

She opened her mouth to answer, paused, then blinked rapidly, her brow creasing as though confused. "Er..." She cleared her throat, frowning more deeply, and massaged her neck. "Um, actually, I haven't decided."

Yasmine nodded at me to keep prodding. It did seem as though something was happening—hopefully the truth serum was beginning to do its thing.

I laced my hands on the huge table as Gus leaned over Olwen's shoulder, and the others stood around us, effectively boxing her in.

I glanced toward the fanny pack in her lap, which bulged with the small jar. "Can I ask what you have there? I thought I saw you collecting something on our hike this morning."

"Death cap mushrooms." Her blue eyes widened so that the whites showed all around them, and she clapped a hand over her mouth.

Yep—the serum was definitely working.

She pulled the jar out of her pocket and set it on the table in view of everyone. Dom leaned over, holding the lantern closer and sure enough, a few little brown mushrooms sat piled inside the glass.

Cho grimaced and edged away from the mommy blogger, while Calvin gawked at her.

"I daresay we can assume you are the one who poisoned Irene Fernsby?" Fitz leveled her with a stern look.

Olwen recoiled, bumping into Gus beside her. "What? No." She shook her head, loosening a few wavy locks. "No way. Why would you think that?"

She seemed genuinely shocked that we'd suspect her of killing Irene.

Leo snorted and crossed his thick arms. "Oh, I don't know, lady, because Irene was killed by death cap mushrooms and you've got a jar of them there?" He threw his hand at the mushrooms sitting on the table.

"Oh... that." Olwen paled and looked down at her hands before shooting us an imploring look. "I get how this looks bad, but that's not why I have these."

"Please, do explain," Gus purred.

Olwen wrung her hands, her lips pressed tight together for a few long moments before she slumped in her seat and flipped open her notebook. "Alright, I'll tell you everything." It was as if she'd been trying to hold back before, but the floodwaters broke. Yasmine and I grinned at each other—this had to be our magic at work. Go witchy sister power!

"My family owns a small farm downstream from here... or at least owned it until recently. It's been in the family for four generations."

"The Feldman Farm," I prompted, and her eyes widened with surprise.

"Yeah."

"We passed the sign on the way in," I explained, leaving out the part about scouring her blog to find her maiden name.

"Oh, right." She propped her elbows on the table and spread her hands, addressing the group of us as a whole. "Last year, my grandpa made a handshake deal with Bobby and Ellie to allow their construction trucks and cranes and various machines to cut through their fields, with the understanding that the Changs would repair any damage." She shook her head. "I know, I know, he should've drawn up a contract, but my family's lived in the area for years and years. It used to be that everyone knew each other and could trust each other's word. For Gramps, this is how business was done in his day."

I grimaced. "Let me guess—Ellie and Bobby didn't follow through with their end of the deal?"

She huffed, the weariness showing in her face. "No. And times have been tough on the farm for years already. Between the large corporate farms pushing out family farmers, low food prices, and dwindling subsidies—my family was barely getting by."

Gus drummed his fingers on the back of Olwen's chair. "What happened, darling?"

She shrugged. "I guess the Changs ran out of money."

I nodded. Bobby had said so himself—that the renovations on the manor house had far exceeded their budget. I understood that was the case for most projects, but seeing how they'd spared no expense in this place, I couldn't help but suspect Bobby's champagne taste had something to do with the overages.

Olwen continued, her jaw set. "They claimed they didn't have any money left to fix the land and repair the fences they'd damaged during construction. That was valuable farmland they trampled all over. It'll take years and years of rehabilitation to make it fertile again." She slumped down, her gaze far away. "Every attempt my grandparents and parents made to collect was stonewalled by Florence, once they brought her on. 'We simply can't pay, sorry. Where's that contract again? Oh, you don't have one...'" Olwen parroted, mimicking Florence's chirpy, bubbly tone.

She set her jaw. "They destroyed the land, left mountains of debris, and worst of all, dumped their refuse into the river—polluting the water and ruining our crops." I could tell that them wantonly sullying this gorgeous stretch of countryside angered Olwen the most, and I had to admit it even made my blood boil a bit.

"Leftover cement, paint, spare parts—all running off into the river." She threw an arm toward the storm raging outside the window and the churning, high waters of the river. She pulled out her phone, clicked through, and then turned the screen around to show us. She scrolled through images of the inside of the garage and stables, with piles of building materials stored in spare stalls and around the Land Rover.

"I've been taking notes"—she tapped her notebook—"and sneaking pictures of their extra materials. I even took samples from their riverbanks and the woods around here, to gather evidence and prove it was the Changs that polluted the river."

I raised a brow. "Is that what the mushrooms are all about then?"

She nodded.

"And the reason you were snooping in Ellie's desk," Fitz added.

Olwen met his gaze. "I'll do whatever it takes. All the farms downstream are suffering from the runoff, but Ellie and Bobby will probably blame it on the storm now. But no —it was them, and I don't intend to let them get away with this." She pressed a hand to her heart. "Our family farm is facing foreclosure due to this pretentious, obnoxious wellness retreat. My older parents and elderly grandparents are losing their homes and livelihoods." She snorted. "And all their lip service to local honey and partnering with farms and the draw of this wildwood—they don't care about any of it. If they did, they wouldn't be actively destroying it."

I blew out the breath I'd been holding. That was messed up. I caught Fitz's eye, and he cleared his throat. "Olwen, I can well understand your anger. As someone whose family has a generational, vested interest in some land not too far from here, I too would feel an obligation to protect it and punish anyone who dared pollute it."

She nodded at him.

He kept his tone gentle, neutral. "Is that what you intended to do, then? Punish them? A death here, on opening weekend, would surely sully the retreat's reputation and perhaps even shut down the business, as they shut down your family's farm."

She scoffed. "No, okay? No." She grabbed her notebook. "I intended to gather dirt and force someone to listen to me." Her nostrils flared as her face flushed with anger. "Florence and Bobby bribed local officials to keep them from looking into the contamination charges."

"Seriously?"

She nodded, and the argument between Ellie and Florence we'd overheard when first checking in returned to me. Florence had been justifying some action by claiming she was "greasing the wheels" like everyone did. That could easily mean bribing an official.

She skimmed through her phone, then turned the screen toward us. A shaky video played of a crowded restaurant, loud with the murmur of conversations and the clink of silverware. The footage zoomed in on a back booth where Florence, Bobby, and an older man in a nice suit dined together. Bobby passed a thick envelope to the older guy, and the video stopped.

"I even caught it on video. Of course, I can't prove it was cash inside the envelope, but that's our local councilman who's got a shady reputation. That, plus everything else I've collected—it paints a picture."

Olwen lifted her chin. "I'm going to gather such a mountain of evidence that the press, officials, police—I don't know who, exactly, but *someone* has to listen." She shrugged. "Besides, murdering someone and merely shutting the business down wouldn't solve the problem." She jabbed the table. "I intend to sue them, get the farm back, and force the Changs to clean up the river." A hint of a smile tugged at the corner of her mouth. "A little public shaming wouldn't hurt, either."

Cho frowned. "Wouldn't want to get on your bad side."

She shot him a sharp look and he raised his hands in surrender. "I'm just saying that's intense. I'm surprised they let you join the weekend."

She smirked. "Well, I didn't tell them who I was. Feldman's my maiden name, so the connection isn't obvious, and Florence didn't do any real research. I approached her with the number of local followers my blog has, and she welcomed me with open arms."

I nibbled the inside of my cheek. If Olwen attended the weekend with ulterior motives, someone else could easily be here with a secret agenda, too. Thanks to the truth serum, we could be sure of one thing—Olwen was not our killer. Which meant the real murderer was still roaming around the manor house with us, in the dark.

21

UPON REFLECTION

"If you'll excuse me..." Olwen rose, scooped up her notebook and other belongings, and then hurried out of the dining room, muttering to herself, "I need to work on oversharing."

After the door swung shut behind her, leaving me and my friends alone at the long table, I winced. "Oversharing wasn't really her fault."

Leo wiggled his fingers at me and Yas, who sat across the table from each other. "You two put a spell on her."

I chuckled, feeling half guilty at using magic to push Olwen into telling us the truth, and half proud that it'd worked.

Yas winked at me. "We make a good team."

We air high-fived across the wide table.

Gus slid into what had been Olwen's seat. "Now what?"

Al looked sheepish. "I hate to say it, but I'm a bit disappointed she *wasn't* the killer." He waved his hands. "Not that I want anyone to be a murderer, but..."

Yas smiled at him, and I nodded. "No, we get it. It'd be satisfying to get this case wrapped up."

"Safer, too," Dom grumbled. He paced on the other side

of the table with his arms folded. "I'd rather not see any more ghosts this weekend."

I nodded. I followed his meaning that if we didn't find the killer, and soon, someone else might be their next victim. It's not like it'd be hard to corner someone in this massive, dark manor home, and with the loud thunder outside, we might not even hear someone call for help. I shuddered at *that* cheery thought. My reluctance to go down that line of thinking gave me the motivation to keep sleuthing.

I rose and paced opposite Dom on my side of the table.

"You two are going to make me dizzy," Gus drawled.

I ignored him. "Let's go over this again. Maybe it'll shake something loose."

"I think everything in Cho's head is already loose." Leo wrapped Cho in a headlock and gave him a noogie as Cho protested and writhed to get away. Dom casually stepped up behind them, and both men immediately separated and sat quietly. I grinned—nobody messed with Dom.

I shook myself mentally and returned to the task at hand. "Every case comes down to means, motive, and opportunity. In terms of means—anyone could have gathered those poisonous mushrooms out here in the countryside, or had them earlier if this was premeditated before the weekend."

"Opportunity?" Fitz prompted.

I paced toward the dark fireplace, the hardwood floors creaking under my steps. It would be nice to have more light, and warmth. Now that the sun had set, the rooms were growing downright chilly. I concentrated my powers on igniting the charred logs, and they burst into flame.

Calvin jumped halfway out of his chair, and I shot him an apologetic smile. "I'll give you a warning next time."

He nodded as he slowly lowered himself back into his seat.

"Opportunity, opportunity," I mused. "Maybe we can at least eliminate some people based on where they were sitting." I lifted a palm. "Because someone had to slip cooked and seasoned poisonous mushrooms onto that plate."

Fitz reached into the inside pocket of his jacket and withdrew a folded piece of parchment. "I have paper if we'd like to sketch it out."

Yas pulled a pen out of her pocket and Fitz passed the paper to her. She quickly outlined the long rectangle of the table, then added smaller rectangles lining each side to represent the chairs.

Leo reached over and tapped the page. "Don't forget our hosts—they were serving."

Along the side of the paper, Yas drew two stick figures and labeled them "Bobby" and "Ellie."

I leaned across the table as everyone else gathered around Yasmine. "Right, Bobby could've added the mushrooms while cooking, and Ellie might've added the mushrooms while serving. Even though they'd have to ignore the damage that a death, much less a murder, would do to their business."

"We're *only* talking opportunity," Gus reminded me.

True.

Yasmine circled Bobby and Ellie's stick figures. "Where was everyone else sitting?"

Bit by bit, we all pieced together the seating arrangement from last night.

"Nathan sat at the top corner, where Minnie's at," Cho recalled.

Yasmine filled in his name.

"Kurt and I sat across from him, with Ellie and Bobby at the head of the table," added Gus.

Down the line we went, adding Leo, Cho, Karine, Janisa,

Irene, Olwen, and Florence down one side, and Dom, me, Fitz, Al, and Yasmine, down the other.

Cho leaned over Yasmine's shoulder. "But remember, Irene and Florence swapped seats so Irene could sit by the fire."

Yasmine added a two-way arrow to indicate the change of spots, then heavily circled the poisoned plate at the very end of the table beside the fire—the one Irene had eaten from and died.

I climbed up on my knees to get a better look from across the table and squinted at the sketch. "So Olwen sat close enough to the plate to sneak something onto it without being noticed."

Yasmine circled Olwen's name. "It could've been Florence, who initially sat at that spot."

Calvin gasped. "You think she poisoned her own plate?"

"Probably not, unless she anticipated Irene wanting to switch seats." Yas shrugged. "But we're listing *everyone* with opportunity."

"I guess we should include Irene herself, then," Leo mused. "I think that's everybody."

Fitz grinned at me. "That quite nicely narrowed down our suspect pool. Good idea, Minnie."

I beamed with pride. "Well, you don't sleuth your way through a few cases without learning something here and there."

"Snoop your way, you mean."

I glared at Gus, who kept his eyes on Yas's sketch and only grinned a tiny bit while pretending to ignore me.

Yasmine made a list of names down the side of the thick parchment. "So we have Bobby, Ellie, Florence, Irene, or Olwen. They're the only ones who touched the plate or sat close enough to add poisonous mushrooms to it."

Leo looked between her and me. "But your potion worked, right? Olwen said she didn't kill Irene."

Yasmine nodded and crossed her name off.

"And I highly doubt that crotchety old woman poisoned herself," Gus lazily rolled his wrist. "That type tends to be too ornery to go easily."

Yas crossed Irene off the list. "That leaves Bobby, Ellie, or Florence."

I nibbled my lip. That meant Kurt was innocent—I already figured as much. And Serena—who didn't eat with us—as well as Nathan, also had to be innocent. Nathan had been sitting exactly where I currently sat, in the seat furthest away from Irene's spot next to the fire.

As I sat there, I tried to imagine last night's dinner from Nathan's perspective. Bobby was in the kitchen, Ellie carrying out plates of food from behind the wall to my left that obscured the door and...

Something slid into place for me as I stared past Yasmine and the guys huddled around her, to the large, gilded mirror hanging on the wall. I caught my own shadowy reflection in the low light, but that wasn't all. In the mirror, I could see around the corner of the wall to the kitchen door. The reflection showed me that small, hidden space between the kitchen and the dining room.

"Guys."

Fitz turned to me, and gradually the others lent me their attention.

I pointed at the mirror. "Look."

They turned and Gus followed my line of sight, but it didn't immediately click for them. I pushed away from the table and leapt to my feet, my heart beating faster now. I was onto something—my witchy intuition tingled and sent zips down my spine. I ran around the short wall, then peeked around it.

"Minnie, now is not the time for hide-and-seek," Gus teased. "Also, you're abysmal at it, we can all see you."

I grinned, barely able to contain my growing excitement.

"Can you, though?" I stepped back in front of the kitchen door, hidden behind the wall. "Can you now?"

"Obviously, not," Cho called. In a lower voice, he added, "Is she okay?"

I rolled my eyes. "I'm fine. Move to where I was sitting."

Some sighs sounded, but everyone shuffled over to the chair, and I waved at them until they caught my reflection in the mirror. Then I mimed holding a plate, and sprinkling something onto it, before rounding the corner. I turned to the others, waiting for their reactions.

"Now she's playing charades," Gus teased, throwing his hands in the air in faux frustration.

I smirked at him. "No. Do you see?"

Calvin shook his head, and I sucked in a breath, trying to organize my racing thoughts in a way that would make sense.

"If Ellie was the one who added the poisonous mushrooms, she would have done it back there, right? With the door closed, Bobby wouldn't have seen her from the kitchen, and the wall hid her from the view of everyone else... almost." I pointed at the chair where Yasmine now sat.

She gasped. "Everyone but Nathan! He could've seen her add the poisonous mushrooms in the reflection of the mirror."

Gus gave me an appreciative grin. "All that snooping does pay off now and then, it seems."

"Sleuthing," I corrected, then grinned. "I think we need to pay Nathan Woods a little visit. He's been acting weird all day—maybe it's because he caught Ellie in the act of poisoning the food."

Cho frowned. "Why wouldn't he say something at the time?"

Yas spun around to face him. "He probably didn't think anything of it until later, after Irene died and we learned about the poisonous mushrooms."

Fitz rose, his dark eyes twinkling. "Cleverly done, Minnie."

My cheeks flushed warm at the compliment.

"Anyone know where Nathan is?" Leo lifted his palms.

Gus rose gracefully, like a cat, and lifted his chin. "My room happens to be beside his. Maybe we'll find him there."

My bestie took the lead as we hurried behind him, lanterns held high, through the lounge and across to the other wing of the house. As soon as we stepped into the hallway that held our rooms, Gus and Fitz exchanged wide-eyed looks, and Leo wrinkled his nose.

"I smell... blood."

The vampires sprinted halfway down the hall, then skidded to a stop in front of what must be Nathan's room with the rest of us running after them. Gus raised his fist to knock but sucked in a breath—the door sat ajar. He pushed it open, and we all crowded in behind Fitz and Gus.

I leaned to the side to peer around them as they came to an abrupt halt. The iron tang of blood now flooded even my own nostrils, and I cringed and brought my hand to my face.

Fitz lifted his lantern, illuminating a body sprawled on the rug. Unmoving and unseeing, Nathan Woods lay in a pool of blood.

22

THE CHASE

My throat grew tight, and I froze in fear as Cho let out a high-pitched scream. Chaos ensued as Calvin's eyelids fluttered and Dom grabbed him by the shoulders just in time to guide him into the nearest armchair before he fainted. Al ushered Yasmine back into the hall with Cho right beside them. Gus and Fitz dropped down beside the unconscious Nathan.

My chest heaved as I waited for their proclamation. Fitz dipped his head close to the man's chest, no doubt listening for any signs of life.

"Is he...?"

Fitz shook his head.

My stomach dropped. Oh no. Another murder, by the looks of all the blood.

Dom bent forward in front of Calvin, gently slapping his cheeks. "Stay awake."

I inched closer to the gruesome crime scene. "How was he killed?" I didn't want to look too closely, but Gus and Fitz gently examined Nathan's body.

"There you are." Dom gave a satisfied nod as Calvin blinked his eyes open and his breath steadied.

My relief at Calvin regaining consciousness was short lived as he sucked in a horrified gasp, let out a strangled cry, and pointed up toward the ceiling over Dom's shoulder.

Dom and Leo lifted their lanterns, and orange light fell on Serena, braced up against the ceiling in the far corner of the room like a horror movie demon.

I screamed, Calvin fully lost consciousness—his head lolling against his shoulder—and even Leo and Dom, who were usually fairly unflappable, yelped and scrambled back.

"Everybody stay calm," the vampire yoga instructor cautioned from her ceiling corner. Her words might've been soothing had her mouth not been smeared with blood.

I turned away, nauseated. Sure, I was used to Fitz and Gus drinking the red liquid, but they sipped it out of donated bags with a straw or from a wineglass. It was downright cultivated. But this? Serena had murdered a man to drink his blood, lips to vein, and it made my stomach wrench.

Muffled cries sounded from somewhere in the house. "Is everyone alright?"

Serena lifted a hand from the wall, the palm red with blood. "I know what it looks like, but I didn't kill him."

Leo let out something between a scoff and a whimper. "You expect us to believe that?"

"I can't believe I trusted you," Cho muttered, peeking back in from the hallway. "You gave me vitamin packets—I thought you were cool."

I shot him a flat look. Now hardly seemed the time.

Serena pointed at Nathan's body. "I found him like that." She gave us a sheepish grin, her fangs protruding over her red lips. "I got a little thirsty."

Gus glared at her. "Whether that's true or not, you've made a real mess."

"Out of the way!" I whirled as Kurt shoved past my friends, stake drawn, and scanned the room. His eyes landed on Serena, then widened momentarily. "Aha! I knew there was a vampire slinking around."

"No!" I lurched forward, reaching for his arm to stop him from attacking before we knew if she'd actually killed Nathan.

But Kurt was quick. I'd never seen him in action before, but it was clear this wasn't his first rodeo with a vampire. In a blink, he vaulted onto the bed, then took a flying leap at Serena. She skittered sideways, pressed up against the ceiling, and Kurt's stake punctured a hole in the plaster wall, right where her heart had been a moment before.

She hissed at him, baring her teeth, and goose bumps crawled up my spine. Kurt, completely unfazed, grabbed the desk chair and flung it up at her. Serena caught it and hurled it back, barely missing him. The chair splintered and flew apart and Fitz jumped in front of me to shield me from flying debris. Serena crawled across the ceiling to escape as Kurt picked up a broken-off chair leg and used it as a second stake, double fisting it.

"Get out!" the hunter barked, his eyes never leaving the vampire. "She's just had fresh blood—she'll be extra quick and strong."

"Kurt, don't—"

But he cut me off. "I've got this Minnie."

Dom threw Calvin over his shoulder like a sack of potatoes, and all my friends jostled with each other in their haste to escape the room that had suddenly turned into a battle ground. Fitz ushered me toward the door, but I couldn't take my eyes off the superhuman—and frankly creepy—way Serena skittered, and the grace and stunning power with which Kurt pursued her.

As I stumbled backwards, guided by Fitz, Gus stood frozen, also seemingly entranced by the epic battle that was thoroughly destroying the room. Kurt hurled his stakes at Serena in fast succession. She dodged the first one, but he'd anticipated her maneuver and the second landed in her thigh.

She howled in pain, and the hairs rose on the back of my neck. "Ow!" she spat at him, yanking the stake out of her leg. "That stings!"

Kurt dipped down to grab another piece of the splintered chair, and Serena seized the moment. She launched herself at him, tackling him to the ground with a force I didn't think the petite yoga teacher was capable of. The wooden leg flew out of Kurt's grasp, and Serena crouched on top of him, pinning down his arms and legs.

"I... didn't... want to... hurt anyone..." Serena ground out as she fought to pin the struggling Kurt down. "But... I have no... love... of hunters." She bared her fangs, her eyes blazing with anger, and slammed Kurt against the floor.

Fitz and I hovered in the doorway, my emotions a jumbled mess. On one hand, I absolutely did not want Kurt to kill Serena. She may be a vampire involved in a cult—probably Darius's—but hadn't Fitz been in the same position not too long ago? Besides, my intuition told me she hadn't killed Nathan, or Irene, for that matter.

On the other hand, inexplicably, I'd grown fond of Kurt. He was someone who hunted people like my friends and me. There was no way I should care about him, much less count him as a friend. But here I was. Despite what he'd been trained by his family to be, he wasn't cruel. He didn't enjoy the hunt, just viewed it as a dirty job somebody had to do. He was actually kind of funny, in his own odd way, and had gone out of his way to help and protect me many times.

"Serena, don't."

I'd lost track of Gus in the scuffle, but he hovered nearby, his intense gaze laser focused on Serena and Kurt. He stood tense, coiled, his hands clenched into fists.

But she was too caught up in the moment to spare Gus a

thought. She dipped her fangs toward the struggling Kurt's neck and—

In a blur, Gus flew across the room and slammed into Serena, knocking her over and pinning her down.

"Get—off me!" she shrieked, struggling under my friend.

I stepped forward, worried about Gus, but Fitz held me close to him. "He's got this," he murmured.

She bared her teeth and hissed, but Gus hissed right back at her. She bucked her hips and knocked Gus sideways, then skittered back up the wall like a spider, but Gus followed right behind her, chasing her around the ceiling and keeping her away from Kurt.

Eventually, it became clear that Serena didn't stand a chance against Gus, even with the fresh blood in her system. She huffed. "I don't know why you're protecting a hunter," she grumbled. "But whatever." With a roll of her eyes, she disappeared in a cloud of smoky purple magic. When it cleared, she'd been replaced by a smallish black bat who squeaked as she flapped out the door over our heads and down the hall.

I looked back at Cho, who gaped at me. "Was that—?"

I nodded and turned back to the scene in the room. Gus dropped from the ceiling and landed gracefully on his feet like a cat, then turned to Kurt. The hunter scrambled to his feet, stumbling a bit, then braced himself against the fireplace. He stared at my friend with his mouth agape. The man who'd gone toe-to-toe with a lithe, agile vampire a moment ago now seemed unable to even form a single word.

I bit my lip. Poor guy. His entire worldview had just been turned upside down. A vampire had not only saved his life, but was—surprise—his lover.

Fitz and I eased back into the room as Gus and Kurt continued to stare at each other.

"You good?"

Gus nodded, not taking his eyes off Kurt. "I think he's in shock."

I felt for my bestie. I could tell he really cared about Kurt. Gus liked to play it cool and aloof, but I knew it would crush him if Kurt outright rejected him for what he was. I edged closer to the two of them. The hunter still hadn't moved.

"Kurt, you doing okay, buddy?"

He only blinked, but I took that as a good sign that he hadn't gone completely catatonic. Maybe I could help smooth this over. But as I moved closer, a bobbing light outside the window caught my eye. I peered through the wet panes at the dark figure scrambling across the muddy lawn with a swinging lantern.

I made out overalls and galoshes—Ellie. I dashed past Gus and Kurt and lowered my face close to the cold panes, wiping away the condensation. She was carrying something in her arms and hurrying toward the stables. It hit me like the lightning zigzagging across the dark sky.

I gasped. "Ellie! It has to be Ellie." I whipped around to address my friends and Fitz. "She killed Nathan because she knew he'd seen her add the poisonous mushrooms—he caught her in the mirror—and she killed him to keep him quiet." I pointed behind me at the window. "She's making a break for it right now!"

I sprinted for the door.

Fitz held up a palm. "Hold now—she won't get far in this weather. All the roads are flooded."

I shook my head at him. "They have a Land Rover, remember?"

Cho peeked into the door and nodded. "Those things are hardcore. They can drive through like a meter of water."

Fitz pressed his lips together—I could tell he didn't like the idea of me chasing a murderer through a thunderstorm at night. But we didn't have much time.

He gestured at the odd standoff going on between Gus and Kurt. "I don't want to leave these two alone."

"Good call." Whenever Kurt's broken brain started to work again, who knew if he'd follow his heart or his life's training and attack my friend. Fitz should be here to keep the peace in case that happened.

I started toward the door again.

"You're not going alone." Fitz's deep voice was hoarse with worry.

"We'll go with her," Dom volunteered, clapping Leo on the shoulder.

The stocky guy squared his shoulders. "Okay, yeah, let's go."

The three of us sprinted down the hallway, their lanterns swinging, and passed a panicked Bobby and Florence along the way.

"There you are!"

"Is everyone alright—we heard screams?"

Leo just pointed behind us, and we kept running. They were not going to love the massive damage to their hotel room, but at least they could call the police to take proper care of poor Nathan's body. Leo, Dom, and I dodged the furniture in the lounge, then threw open the french doors and dashed out into the lashing rain.

23

TIPPING POINT

Rain stung my face as I ran—or tried to—across the soggy lawn. I slipped and caught myself, my hand sinking into the cold, wet mud. Leo and Dom quickly outstripped me in the race toward Ellie.

"Oi!" Leo shouted, his voice blown back by the wind. "Hold up!"

She spun back, her lantern lifted, peering into the dark. Ellie held a bundle clutched to her chest against her rain slicker. She blanched as she caught sight of us and scurried faster toward the stables—and the connected garage behind them that housed the Land Rover.

While I was glad that the guys were catching up to her, I lamented that they were the ones with the lanterns.

I scrambled my way through the dark, following their two bobbing orange lights, and the one further ahead—Ellie. She disappeared inside the stables. What was in that bundle she carried? A new worry tightened my stomach—hopefully it wasn't a gun or some other weapon.

I sloshed onward, my muscles burning as I trudged across the half-submerged lawn. Lightning streaked through the sky, some far off across the hills, others alarmingly close.

Thunder boomed, deafeningly loud, and in the breaks between claps, the churning river gurgled somewhere in the dark to my left.

I looked up in time to catch Leo and Dom dash inside the stable. I worried about them in case Ellie was armed, but they were two buff dudes. Hopefully, they'd be strong enough to overpower her.

I stumbled up to the door of the stables. Panting for breath, shivering, and soaked to the bone, I slipped inside. Shadows loomed, but no sign of Leo, Dom, or Ellie. I swept my sopping wet hair back from my face and staggered forward.

Rain pounded on the tin roof, a raucously loud percussion. I wouldn't be able to hear anyone coming over the noise, and though I wanted to call out for my friends, they'd never hear me.

As my eyes adjusted, I spotted a faint orange glow coming from one of the last stalls up on the left. I crept forward, scuffing hay underfoot. Where was everybody? A horse poked its head over the low door and whickered, nearly giving me a heart attack. I flashed my eyes at the cute guy's big brown eyes. Normally, I'd be the first in line to rub its nose, but this was not the time to be jumping out at me in the dark.

I'd nearly reached that last, glowing stall, when the world went black. Magic tingles danced down my spine, and in my mind's eye I viewed myself as if from overhead, sneaking through the stables. Ellie jumped out from the next stall on the right and swung a shovel right at my head.

With a gasp, I lurched back into my body in real time. I whirled to my right as Ellie leapt out from behind the stall wall. I ducked as the shovel whooshed over my head, then straightened, my heart pounding in my chest. Thank goodness for that spontaneous vision.

Ellie growled in frustration, then swung at me again. I leapt back, barely dodging the shovel.

Ellie shuffled in front of me, jabbing at me with the tool to keep me back. She inched backward toward the doorway. "Stay away or you'll end up like your friends."

My stomach twisted, and I followed her gaze to that last, glowing stall. Dom and Leo lay, unmoving, on a pile of hay, their lanterns tossed in beside them. A hard lump formed in my throat. They'd better only be knocked out—I couldn't bear to imagine how I'd feel if she'd done worse.

I lunged sideways and scooped one of the lanterns up, holding it aloft to see better.

After the initial fright for my friends, hot anger welled up in my chest, and I set my jaw. No way was I letting this woman escape. She'd killed two people and injured my friends. She was going down.

With more distance between us now, Ellie tossed the shovel aside and unwrapped the bundle she held pinned under one arm. She glared at me and brandished a long, sharp-looking kitchen knife in my direction. "I told you—back off!"

I squared my shoulders. I was unarmed—but I had my magic. I made a fist, then stretched my free hand at my side. I was still pretty new at using my powers, but I'd just had a powerful vision that saved me from taking a shovel to the head. It gave me a little boost of confidence.

"Is that the knife you used to kill Nathan?"

Her eyes widened in the orange light of the lantern. Maybe I could fluster her enough to cause her to make a mistake. I considered trying to tackle her but didn't feel like getting stabbed tonight. I'd have to think of another way to stop her.

I pressed on. "You had to kill him. He saw you add the poisonous mushrooms to the dish in the dining room mirror."

She scoffed, her lips curling into a wry smile. "Astute. I'm impressed."

I followed Ellie through an open doorway. The rain quieted, and the pungent smells of fertilizer and gasoline mixed to form a familiar garage smell. She edged toward the metal garage door and lifted it, all the while keeping the knife point trained at me. The roar of the river, wind, and rain all came rushing back in through the wide opening.

Ellie nodded, shouting to be heard over the elements. "Nathan came to me earlier today, demanding money to keep quiet. I guess he put two and two together once Irene was found dead. He realized he'd seen me poisoning her last night."

The way she talked about it seemed almost casual. She pulled keys out of her overall pockets and pressed the fob. The Land Rover behind her beeped, its headlights flashing in the darkness.

"Why didn't he go to the police?" I yelled at her.

She shrugged, her wet wavy locks framing her face. "Guess he actually got fired from *Journey* magazine and his personal travel blog wasn't paying the bills. Turned him a bit opportunistic, it seems."

Was she judging him? That was rich, from a murderer.

"He demanded more than we'd originally agreed on this afternoon, and when I pushed back, he got squirrelly—then he actually did threaten to go to the police." She grimaced. "Can't be having that now, so I had to take care of him." She mimed drawing the knife across her throat. Considering it was the weapon she'd actually used to kill Nathan, it was more than a little macabre.

She patted around behind her, found the handle, and threw open the driver-side door.

"Why are you doing this?"

She paused with one foot up on the door frame. "I meant to kill Florence." Her eyes gleamed with hate. "It'd be great—I could frame my husband for killing his mistress. And the police would either rule it murder or accidental. Either way, he's going down, because no one's going to want to eat from a chef who killed someone out of negligence."

She shook her head, looking briefly remorseful. "But I guess she switched places when I wasn't looking, and I killed Irene instead." She shrugged. "That was my fault—I was a bit flustered, as you can imagine, and didn't notice that they'd swapped positions. My first murder; I'm bound to make some mistakes."

Did she expect me to find this relatable?

She gestured with her hands, swinging the knife around. "I feel bad Irene had to die... and Nathan, but I figured Bobby poisoning an old lady out of negligence, then stabbing a writer who threatened to leave him a bad review, would tank this place and get me my revenge just as well as killing Florence would."

I shook my head at her, disgusted. "But it's your business too."

Her expression grew stony. "It was supposed to be. But that's Bobby—it's always all about him. This was supposed to be our fresh start, but he simply couldn't keep his hands to himself." She gave a humorless chuckle. "I've always taken a back seat to Bobby and his wishes and desires. Add to that the renovations, putting all our money into this endeavor, moving away from all my friends in London—can you blame me if I snapped?"

She certainly had snapped. This lady was unhinged.

She smiled. "I wanted revenge. I wanted to punish Bobby—him and his mistress and his precious business. I wanted to ruin everything he loved." She giggled. "And I have."

Some quote about "a woman scorned" floated through my mind.

With a little hop, Ellie climbed up into the tall vehicle.

The engine rumbled to life, and she rolled the window down to talk to me. It was bizarre how casually she was treating this.

"But I know what you did." I shook my head. "Even if you escape the police, no one's going to blame Bobby for killing Irene."

She flipped a hand as if that didn't matter. "Bulbrook Grove's reputation is ruined, either way. Two murders opening weekend? No one thinks that's relaxing." She draped her elbow over the frame and stuck her head out. "Also, you don't have to tell on me." She raised her brows. "Woman to woman, you know what it feels like to be betrayed by a man, I'm sure. We all do."

My stomach clenched. My ex-husband, Desmond, had cheated on me and basically kicked me out to fend for myself without a job or place to live. In fact, I'd have had to leave the country entirely if it weren't for Fitz hiring me at the tearoom. I could sympathize with Ellie—infidelity could be devastating.

"I'll run. You know I'm not going to hurt anyone else—this was about revenge on Bobby. He deserved it!"

I hesitated for a fraction of a second. I did feel for Ellie in some ways. It'd be nice if people like Bobby got what they deserved when they hurt the people closest to them. But like I'd cautioned Kurt not to stake Serena, killing wasn't the way to get justice. Besides, ultimately, it wasn't Bobby who'd paid the steepest price.

"No." I stared up at Ellie. "You could've walked away and sued him for divorce and won assets." I threw my hands up. "You could've even embarrassed him online or in the press if you wanted to get petty—but murder?" I shook my head. "There's no justification for it. Besides, it was Irene and Nathan who lost their lives at *your* hand—innocent people."

Ellie rolled her eyes. "I already told you, I feel bad about that." She lifted her palm. "Come on, though, Irene didn't have many years left and was a bit obnoxious. And Nathan tried to blackmail me—he was hardly innocent."

I gaped at her. Any momentary sympathy I'd felt for her went right out the window.

"'Bye." Ellie waved at me, then rolled up her window.

"No!" I dashed forward, but she floored it and zoomed out the open garage door into the storm.

I chased after her as she drove parallel to the swollen river, but despite skidding a bit on the muddy lawn, she quickly outpaced me, and I jogged to a stop. She'd be caught—wouldn't she? I shivered, blinking against the downpour. Maybe not. With the flooding as bad as Prescott described and the police tied up with weather-related emergencies, it might be a few days before a proper search could be made. By then she might be out of the country and long gone.

No—I had to stop her. But how?

Her red taillights were fading into the dark as she made her escape. I flexed my fingers. Magic. I was a witch. I glanced at the river and grinned. A water witch, in fact.

I closed my eyes, shivering, and focused on the river. It gurgled and churned, swollen with the rains. It was pure, wild power. I gasped as I drew its energy through me, feeling jittery and electric, like I'd chugged a few shots of espresso.

I opened my eyes, found her almost extinguished tail lights in the distance, and pulled with my magic. I coaxed the river to surge up over the bank and slam into the Range Rover, so hard it swept it up and tipped it sideways. "Ha!" I clenched my fist, feeling incredibly powerful for a lovely moment.

But as quickly as it'd come, all that energy flooded out of me, and I swayed on my feet, completely drained.

"Minnie? Minnie!"

Had I really heard my name, or was it the rush of the wind and river playing tricks on me? I peered in the direction of the manor house, barely making out a few balls of orange light through the curtain of rain. I grinned and cupped my hand to my mouth. "Fitz!"

I raised my lantern and stumbled toward the others. My vampire beau rushed up to me, supernaturally fast and nimble in this crazy deluge. He squeezed my shoulders. "You okay? Where are Leo and Dom? Where's Ellie?"

I fought to catch my breath, and my teeth chattered with cold and exhaustion, which made it hard to speak. I pointed at the stables. "She—she hit them in the head—I think—with a shovel."

He shrugged out of his coat and draped it over my shoulders. The rain soaked his white shirt, the fabric clinging to his muscled chest. I shook myself—focus, Minnie. I blinked through the rain at him. "I tipped the Range Rover over." I pointed further down the river toward the now vertical tail lights.

He swept the wavy lock that was plastered to his forehead back and gaped at me. "You did that?"

I smirked. "Witch powers—but someone should probably make sure she doesn't escape." Not that it'd be easy to with the car sideways like that.

"Right." Fitz put his arm around my shoulders and guided me back toward the house. We passed a grim-looking Gus. "Can you check on Leo and Dom? They're injured."

"In the barn." I winced at my bestie. "You and Kurt okay?"

He quirked a brow. "Remains to be seen."

Fitz hugged me closer to his side, both of us soaked through. "I'll fill you in later." He handed me off to Yasmine at the top of the stairs, then jogged off with Cho and Al to retrieve Ellie from the vehicle.

Yasmine ushered me into the lounge and snapped her fingers. A fire roared to life in the fireplace. "Let's get you warm."

I gave her a shaky smile. "Thanks. And dry, ideally."

"Definitely." She beamed at me. "I saw what you did with the river. That's some high-level witchery—I'm impressed." She hurried off to find me a towel, and I dropped to a sit on the rug in front of the crackling logs, not caring that a small puddle was forming around me.

A noise sounded in the dark lounge behind me. The hairs rose on the back of my neck, and I whipped my head around as a dark figure lurched upright from the chaise.

I screamed, and Calvin turned to face me, wide-eyed. I pressed a hand to the chest of my soaking wet shirt and gaped at the freckled butler. I'd had no idea he was lying back there. Dom had probably set him there to recover from his faint. Still, he'd scared me nearly half to death.

"What am I doing out here?" Calvin pressed a hand to his head and frowned, looking around the room with a befuddled expression. "What'd I miss?"

24

KURT

I slept fitfully that night while Gus and Fitz kept watch over Ellie. She'd been trapped when I used my magic to overturn her vehicle but was otherwise unhurt. Thankfully, Dom and Cho recovered consciousness in the stables, and despite some massive headaches, were back on their feet before I'd gone to bed.

Finally, in the gray, early morning light, DIs Prescott and O'Brien arrived at the house in a utility vehicle of their own. Though the roads were still flooded out here in the country, the rain had died down to a drizzle, and the wind subsided. We all gathered together in the lounge, most of us in our pajamas, robes, or loungewear, though Fitz and Gus were, as usual, dressed to the nines in their own ways.

Dark bags hung under Florence's and Bobby's eyes, and Kurt sat alone in the corner, seemingly still in shock. We'd searched the whole manor house last night, and it seemed Serena had fled. Janisa, Karine, and Olwen sat scattered about the room, looking understandably shaken. My stomach clenched as paramedics wheeled a body bag—Nathan—past the doorway into the foyer. The detective inspectors had just walked a handcuffed Ellie out to secure her in the back of their vehicle.

I squeezed Fitz's hand, then rose and sat beside Gus on a velvet loveseat, wrapping my fluffy robe around me. He hadn't taken his eyes off Kurt. I gently patted my bestie's back.

"How're you doing?"

He shot me a wry smile, his eyes bloodshot and posture weary. This was way past Gus's bedtime, and it'd been a draining night.

I lowered my voice, my gaze on Kurt. He'd been staring out the window and hadn't blinked for a while. "What's up with him? He looks... shook."

Gus snorted. "Indeed." He shook his head and looked down at his pale hands in his lap. "I... spoke with him last night. I hate to admit it, but I have real feelings for the man." He gave a humorless chuckle. "This would all be so much simpler if I didn't."

I gave him a tight grin. "Isn't it always the way?"

He let out a wistful sigh. "I think he has feelings for me too, which is understandably confusing for a fellow who's been raised his whole life to hate vampires, so... there's that."

I kept rubbing his back, my voice low. "I *know* he cares for you. If I couldn't see as much by watching you two together, he told me so yesterday after I caught you canoodling in the hot tub."

Gus grinned, but his smile quickly dropped.

"Where's he at with this then?" I'd half expected Kurt to launch an attack on Gus or confront me about being friends with a vampire. I'd imagined the revelation of Gus's true nature going a lot of different ways, but this silence from Kurt? Never would've predicted it, which made me uneasy. What would happen when he snapped out of... whatever this was?

Gus gestured at the hunter in the corner. "He hasn't spoken a word since last night."

Wow. He really was shell-shocked.

"I explained that this was weird for me too," Gus continued. "I told him he had some false notions about vampires that I'd be happy to clear up for him."

I raised my brows. "And?"

Gus shook his head. "He didn't respond—at all. I'm not even sure if he actually heard me."

I blew out a breath. Hoo boy. This was a tricky, weird, and potentially dangerous situation. "Have you considered glamouring him to forget?" Vampires could exert a sort of charismatic influence over humans to change their perception of events and even tweak their memories.

Gus squirmed in his seat and cleared his throat. "I'd rather not." He turned to me, his blond brows drawn. "I know this puts us all at risk but... if I do that, it'll break his trust forever. I know it's foolish, but I still harbor some hope that he'll come around."

My throat grew tight. I hoped so, too. I wanted that for my friend. But Kurt had been hunting vampires all his life. It was a family tradition, an integral part of his identity. While I was sure he cared for Gus, I didn't harbor much optimism that he'd choose my friend over everything he knew.

Gus pressed his lips together. "We'll use it as a last resort."

I nodded, relieved that he was willing to alter Kurt's memory if needed. I just hoped it didn't come to that. "I have faith in you."

My bestie patted my hand.

Prescott and O'Brien strode back into the house and cleared their throats to get our attention. The quiet murmur of conversation died down as everyone turned to them.

"We'll be taking everyone's statements," Prescott said,

pulling his phone from his pocket. "Minnie, a word? Kurt, you too?"

Gus squeezed my shoulder as I rose. Kurt actually stood as well, sweeping his trench coat behind him. So he *wasn't* totally comatose. My stomach clenched with nerves as we approached the detectives. Would Kurt betray us to Prescott? I gave Fitz, then Yasmine, significant looks. If so, we'd have to scramble to keep this under wraps. Some magic and glamouring would be called for, and stat.

O'Brien, Prescott's grizzled partner, glared at the other detective, then at me. I waved and gave him a bright smile, which I was sure he hated.

"Miss Wells, always at the scene of a crime." His gravelly voice and intelligent, piercing eyes still struck fear in me, but I tried not to let on.

"Surely it's not *always*."

Prescott grinned at me, then ushered Kurt and me down the hallway into Ellie's office and closed the door behind us. I fidgeted with the tie of my robe, trying to catch Kurt's eye to get an idea of how this was going to play out, but he refused to look at me. My skin crawled with nerves, and I scratched my shoulder, anxious to get this over with.

Prescott sat on the edge of the big wooden desk and folded his arms. "You two doing alright? I'm guessing there's more to this story?"

I shot another worried look up at Kurt. Bags hung under his eyes and his stubble and mussed hair made him look a little wild. I set my jaw, bracing for the worst.

Prescott gestured at Kurt. "You texted me something about vampires, right?"

Chills shivered down my spine, and my stomach lurched. Here it came. I had to be ready to call for help, or plead with them, or—

Kurt spared me a quick glance before he reached into his pocket. His throat bobbed. "I, uh—I found one of these."

He pulled out the vitamin packet I'd given him and handed it to Prescott, who studied it.

"What's this?"

Kurt looked down at his combat boots, his tone flat. "It contains dried vampire blood. I think it's connected to the vampire cult in Bath but, uh... didn't find anything further."

"So... no vamps here, then?" Prescott frowned, doubtful.

I held my breath as I waited for Kurt to answer.

The hunter turned away. "No vamps." He cleared his throat. "If you'll excuse me." He whirled and disappeared into the hall, closing the door behind him. His heavy footsteps died away.

Prescott scoffed. "What's up with him?"

I gaped after Kurt, speechless. Gus was right—for now, at least. Kurt hadn't ratted us out. I wasn't sure what that meant for the future, but at this moment, I couldn't keep the smile off my face as I turned back to Prescott. "Um..." I smiled broader. "Long weekend."

The detective inspector pressed his lips together. "Hmm."

I lifted my palm. "Oh, uh, I will say, it was Ellie alone who killed Irene and Nathan, but you should also talk to Olwen, the mommy blogger." I gestured with my thumb over my shoulder. "Bobby and Florence aren't exactly innocent. Bulbrook Grove's been padding local officials' pockets and polluting the river—they put Olwen's family's farm out of business."

Prescott's eyes grew wide. "What?" He pulled out his phone and tapped in some notes. "I'll look into that. Anything else?"

I'd already filled him in on the most important points when he'd first arrived this morning, explaining Ellie's motive and how the chase last night had played out—minus the magic, of course.

"Oh—one other thing. I'm not sure if this is a criminal

matter, but I'm pretty sure Janisa Davies faked having and beating cancer in order to get brand deals and hawk her enema teas."

The detective gaped at me for a moment before typing more notes as he muttered to himself. "Yeah, you know, that might constitute fraud. Thanks—we'll look into it."

I nodded. "I think that's it."

"You've been busy." His expression softened. "You know, I'm sure you're exhausted. Maybe you'll think of something else later? We could grab a drink, tonight or tomorrow maybe, and catch up if—"

"Nope." I hurried to the door. "Thanks, but I'm sure there's nothing else." I dashed out into the hallway, practically running away from Prescott's latest advances. I'd probably have to address his feelings for me at some point, but for now, I'd dealt with my fair share of confrontations. As I rushed back into the lounge, my friends all shot me tense, questioning looks. Had Kurt exposed them? Were their secrets safe?

I gave a double thumbs-up and an audible sigh of relief sounded around the room. Gus grinned down at his hands, and I plopped down on the sofa next to Fitz, full of happy relief.

25

COZY

Later that afternoon, Gus drove us back to his place and immediately crashed. Poor guy had been through the wringer and stayed awake way longer than he normally did. I was exhausted too, but oddly wired. My mind wouldn't stop working over the weekend's events and the lingering questions. Would Kurt continue to protect Gus's secret, or would he expose us to Prescott? Could the two of them ever work this out? Was Serena really part of Darius's nest, and where had she fled to?

Instead of leaving to return to his own crumbling manor home, Fitz hesitated in the living room of Gus's historic townhouse.

"Care for a walk? I'd like to check on the cafe and... well, I've got something else in mind, as well."

I happily accepted Fitz's suggestion, looping my arm through his as we walked through the wet streets of Bath. Nothing in the heart of the city had suffered from the floods, but I'd gathered that in the hills and more rural areas, the storm had been quite destructive, and crews were still working to rescue stranded people from their homes and vehicles.

We'd have been stuck in Bulbrook Grove for another day or two at least, but Yasmine and I put our powers together and managed to clear the deepest mud and flooding along the roads, enough for everyone to drive back to town. It'd taken every last ounce of magic I had in me, but I'd been motivated. No way did I want to spend one more night in that creepy retreat. What a shame, too, because it was beautiful, with so much potential. But a couple of murders, a power outage, and being trapped with a killer could really color your impression of a place.

Fitz held his black umbrella overhead, the rain lightly tapping at the fabric as we strolled the bustling Saturday evening streets.

I sighed. "I feel like I need a vacation from our vacation."

Fitz shot me a mysterious look and merely nodded. I could tell he was up to something but didn't have the energy to push it. I'd let whatever it was be a surprise.

We soon reached the tearoom, where the contractor and a few construction workers bustled about with tool belts slung around their hips. I waited in the foyer as Fitz discussed the renovations with the head guy for a few minutes before returning to my side.

"Well?"

He gave me a small smile. "Everything's going well. They should be wrapped up by tonight, maybe tomorrow morning at the latest—the flooding didn't affect anything."

I let out a sigh of relief. "That's great news!" I raised my brows. "So, do you want to open for service tomorrow?"

"Actually, I had something I'd like to propose to you."

I smirked, intrigued. "Oh?" I rose and once again took Fitz's arm as he led me back outside and we strolled toward the river.

Rain pattered against the umbrella as cars swished by on the slick streets. "We were supposed to be gone another night, and Mim was expecting to watch Tilda a little longer, right?"

My smile broadened. "Right. What are you thinking?"

He fought a smile, and my excitement grew as he stayed tight-lipped. "Fitz?" I squeezed his arm, my curiosity piqued.

"Hold on, we're just about there." I did my best to be patient. We stopped at the next corner, and he lifted his chin toward the gorgeous, three-storied Georgian building catty corner to us. It sat at the edge of the river, its striped awning and the golden light spilling out of its windows cozy and beckoning in the evening rain. I squinted to make out the gold lettering above the door.

"The Bath Luxury Spa?" I smiled up at my boyfriend.

He nodded, his dark eyes twinkling. "It's a boutique hotel and spa with elegant soaking pools and fantastic services." His cheeks flushed a little pink. "At least that's what Mrs. Crenshaw, one of our regulars, said. She told me all about it a few months ago, and I filed it away, thinking I might want to take you there someday."

I gasped, suddenly feeling downright giddy. "Is today that someday?"

He gazed tenderly down at me. "It is. I—I've been doing a lot of reflecting. And I already share so much with you. You know me better and deeper than anyone I've ever met, in my long life." His throat bobbed. "I know I've hesitated a bit with, er, taking some next steps in our relationship because of the morals and rules I grew up with. But I've come to realize that for myself, for our relationship, I don't believe what anyone else, or society at large, dictates should shape our course." He tenderly cupped my cheek. "It's more important how I feel about you. And, I *feel* open to you Minnie—in soul, mind, and body."

Happy tingles zipped down my spine. I might swoon right there on the street corner.

He cleared his throat. "No pressure intended—but I'd like to have a real romantic night alone with you, Minnie. Just the two of us."

My face grew warm as I beamed up at him. "I want that too."

He tipped his head to the side. "Well, us and the massage therapist I booked for you."

"You booked me a massage?" Was my boyfriend an angel?

He arched his brow. "And a facial."

My mouth literally fell open. "Yep, you're an angel. I'm in heaven."

He chuckled, and we started across the street, arm in arm. I was going to get that relaxing, cozy, romantic weekend with my vampire boyfriend after all. The nerves were still there, but they'd morphed into giddy excitement as we neared the striped awning and the pampering that awaited us. Most of all, I looked forward to a night alone with Fitz—my considerate, strong, and dashingly handsome love. Whatever next steps we took, we'd take them together and move at the right pace for us.

All those issues with Kurt, Gus, Darius's vampire cult, and Prescott faded to the background—they were problems for a different day. In the meantime, I intended to fully enjoy my time with Fitz.

∼

Think Minnie's magical adventures with Fitz and the tea room are over? No chance...

CLICK HERE TO grab your copy of ***Tea Die For*** so you can keep reading the Magical Tea Room Mysteries today!

And make sure you're on Erin's newsletter list, so you

hear all about the monthly deals, giveaways, and new releases *and* get your exclusive prequel for FREE!

CLICK HERE to subscribe to get your free prequel!

GET YOUR FREE PREQUEL!

It's All Hallows Eve, and the fortune-telling festivities abound at a magical party near charming Bath, England. Only no one predicted that the coven leader would be poisoned! Now, new witch, Minnie and her vampire bestie, Gus, must catch the killer before Gus's secret gets out.

Download Once in a Brew Moon for FREE to solve a mystical murder today!

OTHER BOOKS BY ERIN JOHNSON

The Magical Tea Room Mysteries
Minnie Wells is working her marketing magic to save the coziest, vampire-owned tea room in Bath, England. But add in a string of murders, spells to learn, and a handsome Mr. Darcy-esque boss, and Minnie's cup runneth over with mischief and mayhem.

Spelling the Tea
With Scream and Sugar
A Score to Kettle
English After-Doom Tea
Steeping Secrets
Save the Last Dance for Tea
Steep With One Eye Open
A Bitter Blend
Tea Die For

The Spells & Caramels Paranormal Cozy Mysteries
Imogen Banks is struggling to make it as a baker and a new witch on the mysterious and magical island of Bijou Mer. With a princely beau, a snarky baking flame and a baker's dozen of

hilarious, misfit friends, she'll need all the help she can get when the murder mysteries start piling up.

Seashells, Spells & Caramels
Black Arts, Tarts & Gypsy Carts
Mermaid Fins, Winds & Rolling Pins
Cookie Dough, Snow & Wands Aglow
Full Moons, Dunes & Macaroons
Airships, Crypts & Chocolate Chips
Due East, Beasts & Campfire Feasts
Grimoires, Spas & Chocolate Straws
Eclairs, Scares & Haunted Home Repairs
Bat Wings, Rings & Apron Strings
* Christmas Short Story: Snowflakes, Cakes & Deadly Stakes

The Pet Psychic Magical Mysteries
A curse stole one witch's powers, but gave her the ability to speak with animals. Now Jolene helps a hunky police officer and his sassy, lie-detecting canine solve paranormal mysteries.

Pretty Little Fliers
Friday Night Bites
Game of Bones
Mouse of Cards
Pig Little Lies
Breaking Bat
The Squawking Dead
The Big Fang Theory

The Winter Witches of Holiday Haven
Running a funeral home in the world's most merry of cities has its downsides. For witch, Rudie Hollybrook, things can feel a little isolating. But when a murder rocks the festive town, Rudie's special skills might be the one thing that can help bring the killer to justice!

Cocoa Curses
Solstice Spirits
Mistletoe Mojo

Magical Renaissance Faire Mysteries
Turkey legs, ale, and murder! Is this supernatural Ren Faire cursed? If you like snarky animals, bold heroines, and a hint of romance, you'll love this humorous paranormal cozy series.

Much A'Broom About Nothing
The Taming of the Broom

Special Collections
Spells & Caramels: The Complete Series Boxset

The Spells & Caramels Boxset Books 1-3
The Spells & Caramels Boxset Books 4-6
The Spells & Caramels Boxset Books 7-10

Pet Psychic Mysteries Boxset Books 1-4
Pet Psychic Mysteries Boxset Books 5-8

Winter Witches of Holiday Haven: The Rudie Collection Books 1-3

Want to hang out with Erin and other magical mystery readers?
Come join Erin's VIP reader group on Facebook: **Erin's Bewitching Bevy**. It's a cauldron of fun!

ABOUT THE AUTHOR

A native of Arizona, Erin loves her new home in the Pacific Northwest! She writes paranormal cozy mystery novels. These stories are mysterious, magical, and will hopefully make you laugh.

When not writing, she's hiking, napping with her dogs, and losing at trivia night.

You can find Erin at her website, **www.ErinJohnson Writes.com** or on **Facebook.** Please email her at **erin@erin johnsonwrites.com**. She loves to hear from readers!

Copyright © 2023 by Erin Johnson

All rights reserved.

No part of this book may be reproduced in any form or by any electronic or mechanical means, including information storage and retrieval systems, without written permission from the author, except for the use of brief quotations in a book review.

Cover design by Lou Harper at Cover Affairs.

Printed in Great Britain
by Amazon